"I've got the perfect solution. Marry me."

Laura looked at Tom as if he were crazy. "How can you joke at a time like this?"

"I've never been more serious in my life. If we're married, we'd be in a better position to protect the girls." As he looked at her, she could see his eyes darken. "Besides, we like each other—at least we did till Saturday. Maybe we can learn to like each other again, right?"

That was no reason to marry, Laura thought. But the safety of the girls.... Before she would agree she had to know what Tom expected. She could feel herself blush as she asked, "If I agree to marry you, I have to know how much...of myself you expect me to give."

For a moment Tom seemed lost in thought. "I promise to never do anything to make you regret marrying me," he finally answered. "As for the rest—" the way he looked at her sent her heart racing "—well, I'll leave that up to you."

Dear Reader,

Welcome to another month of wonderful stories at Harlequin American Romance—where you'll find more of what you love to read. Every month we'll bring you a variety of plots from some of the genre's best-loved authors. Harlequin American Romance is all about the pursuit of love and family in the backyards, big cities and wide-open spaces of America!

This month you won't want to miss *A Cowboy's Woman*, the continuation of Cathy Gillen Thacker's series, THE McCABES OF TEXAS. This family of bachelors is in for some surprises when their parents take to matchmaking. And talented author Muriel Jensen brings us *Countdown to Baby*, the second book in the DELIVERY ROOM DADS series. In this three-author, three-book series you'll meet the McIntyre brothers of Bison City, Wyoming. They're in a race to see who'll have the New Year's first baby.

Also this month is Mollie Molay's *Daddy by Christmas*, a compelling story of blended families— just in time for the holidays. And Mindy Neff wraps up her TALL, DARK & IRRESISTIBLE duo with *The Playboy & the Mommy*.

Please drop us a note to tell us what you love about Harlequin American Romance and what you'd like to see in the future. Write to us c/o Harlequin Books, 300 East 42nd Street, 6th Floor, New York, NY 10017.

Happy reading!

Melissa Jeglinski
Associate Senior Editor

Daddy by Christmas

MOLLIE MOLAY

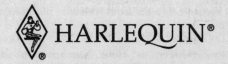

HARLEQUIN®

TORONTO • NEW YORK • LONDON
AMSTERDAM • PARIS • SYDNEY • HAMBURG
STOCKHOLM • ATHENS • TOKYO • MILAN • MADRID
PRAGUE • WARSAW • BUDAPEST • AUCKLAND

To Debra Matteucci
who has an understanding heart,
And to mothers everywhere.

ISBN 0-373-16799-7

DADDY BY CHRISTMAS

Copyright © 1999 by Mollie Molé.

Visit us at www.romance.net

Printed in U.S.A.

ABOUT THE AUTHOR

After working for a number of years as a Logistics Contract Administrator in the aircraft industry, Mollie Molay turned to a career she found far more satisfying—writing romance novels. Mollie lives in Northridge, California, surrounded by her two daughters and six grandchildren, many of whom find their way into her books. She enjoys hearing from her readers and welcomes comments. You can write to her at Harlequin Books, 300 East 42nd St. 6th Floor, New York, NY 10017.

Books by Mollie Molay

HARLEQUIN AMERICAN ROMANCE

Prologue

The auditorium lights dimmed and the music of Tchaikovsky's *Nutcracker Suite* began. The curtains parted and the stage lights slowly came on, including the multicolored lights on a huge Christmas tree at the back of center stage. The fairy tale ballet the school children had been practicing for months began.

Laura Edwards, the proud mother of the Sugar Plum Fairy, sat forward in her seat, the better to see her daughter, Carly. She could see her daughter's eyes sparkle, her lips curve in a wide, welcoming smile as she glanced over her shoulder.

Laura caught her breath when another identically clad little fairy joined her daughter and the girls toed and twirled around the stage to the joyous music of the "Dance of the Sugar Plum Fairy."

But it wasn't only their costumes that were identical. The girls themselves—right down to their auburn hair—were exact.

"Aren't they adorable?" the woman seated next to Laura commented softly. "Twins! I must say, little girls don't come any cuter than that."

Laura sat stunned for a long moment. Was it her

imagination that saw two almost identical children dancing together? Apparently not, after her neighbor's comment. Unable to account for the similarity, Laura slowly sat back in her seat. Her gaze followed the children until they disappeared.

How could another little girl resemble her own daughter so closely when Carly was her only child?

Tom Aldrich smiled proudly when his daughter, Beth, dressed as a Sugar Plum Fairy, danced into view and joined the other small dancer. When he noticed their striking resemblance, he checked the program. There was his daughter, but who was Carly Edwards?

If he hadn't seen it with his own two eyes, he never would have believed how alike the two girls looked. Both girls resembled his ex-wife, Jody—down to their green eyes and curly auburn hair.

Impossible! Beth was his and Jody's only child.

Throughout the remainder of the presentation, questions without answers tumbled through his mind. He remained staring at the stage until a polite cough told him he was holding up the line of people waiting to exit the row of seats. Muttering his apologies, he moved into the aisle. He felt stupid at his runaway thoughts, but he couldn't help himself. Considering how closely the two girls resembled each other, how could they not be related?

Clasping the tiny nosegay he'd brought for Beth's debut, he shook his head and started to make his way backstage. Lost in thought, he collided with the woman who had been sitting across the aisle from him. He'd noticed her fresh good looks and happy smile before the program began, and a quick glance at her ringless finger when she brushed her hair away from her eye had told him she was probably single. In another time and place, he would have spoken to her by now.

He grasped her arm to keep her from falling, but not before she stumbled against him. Her head came comfortably under his chin; her chestnut hair fell to her shoulders in soft, graduated lengths. Under her jacket, she was just as soft as he'd imagined she would be, and, close up under the auditorium lights, far prettier. A faint scent of lilac clung to her.

"Sorry," he said with a sheepish smile. "I guess I was in too much of a hurry to get backstage. My daughter, Beth, was one of the Sugar Plum Fairies. This was her debut performance as a dancer." He indicated the tiny nosegay. "I was on my way backstage to bring her this to celebrate the occasion."

He was about to introduce himself when, to his surprise, she managed a distracted smile before she backed away. With a murmured apology, she rushed down the aisle to the stairs leading backstage.

Puzzled, Tom followed. His experience as an undercover INS detective had taught him it took all kinds of people to make up the world—and that those with something to hide couldn't look you in the eye. What could he have said to make this woman turn away so abruptly?

Beth rushed into his arms when she spotted him. "Daddy, wasn't the show cool?"

"It sure was, sweetheart," Tom answered as he bent to kiss her pert, upturned nose. He handed her the small nosegay with a flourish. "And you were the coolest one of all."

"No, I wasn't, Daddy. Carly was cool, too! I want you to meet her." She gazed around the stage crowded with adoring parents until she broke into a happy smile, grabbed his hand and tugged him after her. "There she is, over there!"

Over there turned out to be with the woman he'd almost knocked over. She was hugging Beth's mirror image.

"Daddy, this is Carly, my very best friend!"

"Well," he said lightly, "any friend of yours is a friend of mine."

He extended his hand to Carly's mother with a rueful smile. "I guess you could say we've already met, but let me introduce myself. I'm Tom Aldrich."

"Yes, we have," she answered with a tight smile. "I'm Laura Edwards and this is my daughter, Carly." Her hand barely brushed his in greeting.

To his surprise, Tom sensed she was unwilling to touch him or to meet his eyes. He could hear the reluctance in her voice, see it in her withdrawn manner.

But what really surprised him had nothing to do with Laura Edwards. It was that, up close, the likeness between his daughter and her friend Carly was stronger than ever.

Chapter One

From the closed expression of Laura Edwards's face, Tom decided this wasn't the time or place to voice his surprise. There was no use looking for trouble, and he had an uneasy feeling that, for some unknown reason, trouble was staring him in the face.

On the other hand, he thought, glancing from one little Sugar Plum Fairy to the other, the similarity between the girls might be simply a chance resemblance, heightened by their look-alike costumes. It was said that everyone had a double somewhere—maybe Carly was Beth's.

He would have dismissed the resemblance more easily if they didn't share a tiny dimple in their chins and a small birthmark at the right side of their lips.

"Well, it's been nice to meet the both of you," he said when the silence became uncomfortable. If he'd been hoping for some encouragement to hang around, it looked as if he'd have a long wait.

With Carly's mother silently regarding him, Tom felt it was time to leave. Any mysteries that could explain the likeness between the girls would have to be explored later, if ever. Right now, he had more important things to think about—like getting reacquainted with his daughter after his month-long absence on assignment for the government.

Beth had remained with his mother after he and Jody had divorced two years ago. He'd been off on assignment until last week and had returned early only after his mother had been taken ill. His mother had recently enrolled Beth in the private Beckwith Day School, but he still had to make arrangements for a permanent housekeeper. Until then, he was in charge, with all the responsibilities that came with the territory.

Maybe he hadn't paid enough attention to Beth and his mother in the past, he thought as he half listened to the flood of Beth's news, but things were going to be different now. From now on, he vowed as he glanced at Beth's glowing face, he intended to be a better father and a more attentive son.

He leaned down to hear Beth's chatter. Wound up like a tight spring, she was telling him all about her newfound friend, Carly. According to Beth, they were in the same grade and had quickly discovered they were a lot alike. To listen to her talk, it sounded as if the two had bonded from the moment they'd met.

He listened dutifully to stories about Carly, but it was Carly's mother, Laura, he couldn't get out of his mind. He'd felt an instant attraction to her and, for a few moments, had hoped it was mutual. It hadn't taken her long to show him how futile that hope had been. But her haunting scent clung to his jacket and reminded him there might be unfinished business between them.

LAURA LEFT THE STAGE as quickly as possible. But not before making sure Tom Aldrich and his daughter were safely out of sight.

She was unable to account for the uneasy feeling that had swept over her when she'd seen the girls together on stage. From the look on his face, Beth's father had been equally taken aback. Now Laura needed time to sort out her reaction.

"Beth is new to the school, isn't she?" she asked her daughter.

"Yes, Mommy, but I feel like I've known her forever."

Laura had to smile. "Forever" was a total of the not quite six short, precious years of Carly's life. "Have you met her mother?"

"No," Carly replied, skipping alongside her, her tiara slipping sideways on her curls. "Beth doesn't have a mommy."

She paused and looked up at Laura. "That's sad, isn't it? She doesn't have a mommy and I don't have a daddy."

Laura squeezed Carly's hand and thought wistfully of Carl, killed in an automobile accident only weeks before Carly's birth. Her heart ached when she thought of how eagerly he'd awaited the birth of his first child, and how proud he would have been to see his daughter dancing on stage tonight.

Unbidden, her thoughts swung to Tom Aldrich who strangely enough resembled her late husband in many ways. About thirty-five, he was also tall, with rugged dark features and a strong, self-assured presence that drew attention. He had certainly drawn hers when she'd bumped into him—until he'd mentioned his daughter and they'd met backstage.

To complicate her mixed reaction to him, there had been the beguiling smile of his that intrigued her. And a sparkle in his golden-brown eyes that recognized her interest and suggested he would like to know her better.

She couldn't afford to dwell on that sparkle or the knowledge that he was the kind of man who could easily turn a woman's thoughts to dreams and passions. Those thoughts were better left in the past where they belonged.

Under other circumstances, things might have been different. But not now. Not after she'd discovered they each had a daughter who looked enough alike to be blood sisters and her mind had gone into a tailspin.

Troubled, Laura shivered in her winter coat.

Outside, the late afternoon air was colder than usual for southern California. Dark clouds drifted overhead and a strong wind whipped through the trees. Leaves were dancing in lazy patterns in the air. With Christmas still less than a month away, it felt as though winter had arrived early.

In spite of Carly's protests that her costume would be crushed, Laura stopped to button her daughter's jacket all the way to her neck. Suddenly, Carly wriggled free to wave at a car leaving the parking lot. "Beth, wait a minute!"

An answering shout turned Laura around. Tom Aldrich had stopped his car just feet away from them and Beth was hanging out the car window waving at them. Laura forced a smile. The meeting she had hoped to avoid was inevitable.

"Mommy," Beth asked in an excited voice, "can I ask Beth to come with us to the park tomorrow?"

Laura bit her lip. Tomorrow was Saturday, a day she and Carly usually spent in the park's arts-and-crafts recreation center. Her first reaction was to tell Carly no, but no doubt Beth had heard Carly asking permission.

She had enough valid reasons for wanting to say no. There had been an instant attraction between them when Tom Aldrich had caught her in his arms after they'd run into each other and he'd held her longer than necessary to keep her from falling. And, more importantly, there had been the puzzled look in his eyes after he'd arrived backstage and seen the girls together.

Two good reasons to stay away from Tom Aldrich, but maybe not enough to keep Carly away from her friend.

Through the car's windshield, she saw Tom Aldrich resting his arms on the steering wheel and gazing at her with a wry crooked smile that seemed to question her. She hid her uneasiness and nodded back. Of the two of them, *he* at least looked pleased.

Visions of spending a morning with him and talking about their children filled her with dread. "All right," she said. "If it's okay with her father." She had to shake off the feeling that nothing good would come of their spending the morning together.

Carly rushed over to the car. "Mommy says it's okay to ask you to play in the park with me tomorrow morning," Carly called to her friend. "Can she, Mr. Aldrich?"

Tom knew that "can she" meant "can we." He

was past the age for parks and too male to want to spend a morning pushing swings, but he remembered the promise he'd made to himself to be a better father. It looked as if spending a morning in the park was included. But at least, he thought gazing at Laura Edwards, it would be with a woman who interested him. Too bad she didn't return the interest.

He sighed, slid out of the car and went around to talk to Carly's mother. From the closed expression on her face, he'd sensed that the last thing Laura wanted to do was spend a morning talking to him.

"If it's okay with you, Mrs. Edwards, it's okay with me."

She nodded. Unless he was mistaken, hesitantly.

"I'll be glad to pick up Beth and take her with us, Mr. Aldrich," she offered. "That way you won't have to come along."

"No, thanks," he answered after a moment's pause. "Tell me how to get to the park and I'll bring her over myself. By the way, since it looks as if we're going to see a lot of each other, how about calling me Tom?"

"Of course," she agreed after a moment's hesitation. He waited for her to invite him to call her by her given name, but it looked as if the invitation wasn't going to be forthcoming.

While he listened to the directions to the park, he decided that as long as they were parents of two children who'd managed to bond so closely, they might as well be friendly.

Laura Edwards puzzled him. She'd been friendly enough when they'd bumped into each other. But she'd sure changed after the four of them had gotten together backstage after the *Nutcracker* performance. He hesitated for a moment, then followed an impulse.

"How about if I call you Laura? It sounds a lot less informal than Mrs. Edwards."

She nodded, but he could see her heart wasn't in it. He didn't know if it was his request that bothered her or his earlier suggestion that they were going to see a lot of each other.

Tomorrow would be a good time to have a heart-to-heart with her and find out what there was about him that made her so reluctant to have him around. Certainly, it was nothing he'd said or done. "Well, so long. We'll see you both tomorrow!"

Laura unlocked her car door and helped Carly in in time to see Tom Aldrich glance out his car window for clearance before he swung away and out of the school's parking lot. His left hand waved a goodbye out the window as his car disappeared around the corner and out of sight.

He left her with mingled reactions. One was an unconscious response to his innate sensuality, another was the sense that told her tomorrow wouldn't be the last she'd see of Tom Aldrich. For whatever the reason, she had the sinking feeling he was about to turn her well-ordered life upside down.

LAURA COULDN'T HELP but be amused at the wary look on Tom's face when he came through the door of the park's activity center. The large, open area decorated for Christmas was a sea of busy children and a cacophony of children's voices. All around, children were chattering excitedly as they made holiday crafts, and in one corner, a small children's orchestra and choir were rehearsing Christmas carols. For a new-comer, the scene must have come as a shock.

She had to give Tom credit for showing up at all.

At her side, Carly jumped up and down and shouted, "Here I am."

"Daddy?" Beth asked, poised to run.

"Go ahead, pumpkin," Tom laughed at her eager-ness to join her friend. "Have fun."

With an apologetic smile in her father's direction, Beth ran across the room and stood beaming at Carly. "What are we going to do today?"

Carly pointed to two easels set up side by side. "I checked out two of them and I saved one for you. You get to draw anything you want."

After a brief exchange of whispered confidences, the girls became lost in a world of their own.

"I have an impression this is a first for you," Laura remarked with a sympathetic look at Tom when he joined her. "It may take some getting used to."

"Yeah," he said with a broad smile. "But thank-fully, a morning at the park isn't what I thought it was going to be."

"Really? What *did* you think it was going to be?"

"From what I heard, sandboxes and swings. I came dressed appropriately." He indicated his worn jeans and a golden-brown turtleneck sweater that matched the hints of gold in his dark eyes. Athletic shoes were on his feet. "To tell the truth, I thought it was kind of cold for sandboxes, but if that's what Beth wanted, I wasn't going to disappoint her."

As far as Laura was concerned, sandbox-ready or no, his clothing fit right in with his rugged features, broad shoulders and his six feet plus of utter masculinity. Caught up by his grin, Laura couldn't help herself. She found herself grinning back.

In the cold light of today, Beth's father seemed harmless enough. What had there been about him yesterday that had made her so reluctant to see him again? Why had she been so quick to think he spelled trouble?

"I'd guess you haven't been around children enough to realize the girls are a little too old for sandboxes," she replied. "Swings are another story. But you're right—it *is* much too cold to play outside. Luckily, Carly's favorite pastime is drawing."

"So is Beth's." He glanced over at the girls, who were absorbed in their drawings. "The kids seem to have more in common than their looks, don't they?"

To his surprise Laura's smile vanished and she turned back to a supply table.

After another quick glance to reassure himself Beth was going to be busy for a while, Tom sauntered over to the table where Laura had begun to nervously sort crayons. He'd figured that whatever it had been about him that had bothered her yesterday was over, but it looked as if he'd been mistaken.

If his law enforcement training hadn't taught him to read people and their thoughts and to judge the truth from the look in their eyes, he might have laid her apprehensive attitude yesterday to his imagination. Somehow, she had been afraid of him then and she was afraid of him now.

She couldn't have known he was an agent for the INS under the genial mask he wore off duty. Nor that his undercover job was to mingle with and bring to justice illegal immigration rings that preyed on all-too-vulnerable targets. Not when he looked like the other few men around. So what was there about him that had frightened her off?

"It looks as if it's going to be an early winter, doesn't it?" he commented to break the silence. No sooner were the words out of his mouth than he began to wonder what in heaven's name he was doing discussing the weather when there were so many other important subjects.

For starters, how did she manage to look so dog-gone attractive while dressed in soft jeans and a long-sleeved denim shirt covered by a Christmas-red sweater? A bulky sweater that covered her to her hips but still managed to make her look sexy as hell.

And since Beth had told him Carly didn't have a dad, he wondered just how available Laura was.

He sighed. At the rate Laura kept freezing up on him whenever they were together, he might never know the answer. He stuck his hands in his pockets and glanced over at Beth. She was happily engrossed in her drawing, her tongue caught between her pursed lips. At her side, Carly was just as immersed in her own masterpiece.

"What do you suppose the kids are drawing that's keeping them so interested?" he wondered aloud.

"I don't know, but I don't suppose it would disturb them if we took a peek." She put the crayons aside and, with a finger on her lips, moved silently to peer over the girls' shoulders.

"Something wrong?" Tom whispered when he saw her face grow still and white. He moved to gaze over Beth's shoulder. He expected to see the stick figures she'd drawn when she was younger, but it looked as if things had changed. Not only had her drawing improved, the figures in her drawing were now clearly human and identifiable by their clothing.

The first frame was of Beth and a male figure that was dressed just as he was. The second, a child with auburn hair and a woman dressed in blue jeans and a red sweater. The third, as yet unfinished, was that of a family enjoying a picnic in the park.

A quick glance at Carly's drawing revealed almost the same scenes.

Coincidence?

An unspoken wish?

Tom took a closer look. The figures in Carly's drawing were labeled Mommy, Daddy, Beth and me. The figures in Beth's were labeled Daddy, Mommy, Carly and me.

No wonder Laura had been taken aback. Seeing himself labeled as Daddy in both pictures darned near floored him, too.

Laura turned away from the easels without comment. The uneasy look he'd seen on her face when they'd been introduced after the Beckwith Day School's *Nutcracker* performance was back.

"Something wrong?"

"I'm not sure," she answered, averting her eyes and busying herself putting the crayons in individual color-coded baskets.

"Not sure about what?"

"It's nothing, actually," Laura answered. "It was just a fleeting thought. It's already gone."

She wanted to tell him she thought it was strange the way the girls' drawings were so much alike. And that the names above the figures were puzzling, too.

To add to the puzzle, when she'd seen them dancing together in the *Nutcracker* performance, it was as though they were two parts of a whole personality. They not only looked alike, their mannerisms were alike, and there even had seemed to be some kind of unspoken communication between them.

She didn't dare voice her thoughts. Not to him. Not without drawing his attention to the details that had begun to bother her from the moment she'd seen the girls together onstage.

Tom glanced thoughtfully at Laura. He caught a glimpse of the troubled look in her eyes and knew there was something wrong.

"If you don't mind my being frank, I have the feeling there's something about me that bothers you," he remarked thoughtfully. "I hope it's not something I said or did. If it is, I'd like to apologize."

"No," she answered quickly, "there's nothing I can talk about. Maybe some other time." She moved away before he could ask any more questions.

"I'm afraid I have that effect on some people," he joked, following her. "I hope I haven't managed to frighten Carly, too."

She shook her head.

When she avoided his eyes, Tom knew he was right.

He'd been willing—no, wanting—to dismiss her earlier reaction to him as a figment of his imagination. But now, all his instincts told him that if ever a person was afraid of something or someone, Laura Edwards with her clenched hands was it.

When he caught her glancing at Carly and Beth,

his gaze followed hers. Suddenly, as if a light had turned on, he began to suspect the truth.

Whatever was bothering Laura didn't have to do with him. It had to do with the girls.

With his eyes on Beth and Carly, he tried to analyze the possibilities. They were two small kids caught up in a newfound friendship. That seemed natural enough. The fact they looked so much alike probably fascinated them as much as it intrigued him. That seemed natural enough, too.

Something else was wrong.

He walked back to study the drawings. What was there that had stilled Laura's smile?

He could lay Carly's labeling him Daddy to wishful thinking, but not his daughter's labeling Laura Mommy. Beth might not remember her mother clearly, but he'd deliberately left a picture of himself, Jody and Beth as an infant in her room so that Beth would know she had a living mother somewhere. Maybe that had been a mistake, but Beth *had* to know Laura wasn't her mother.

Still, the labels in the drawings shouldn't have been that significant to bother Laura. Not unless there was more to her reaction than met the eye.

He walked slowly back to the table and stood beside it until Laura looked up at him. Vulnerability showed in her troubled hazel eyes. He had a wild, crazy, irrational urge to comfort her, for what, he wasn't sure. She'd only think he'd lost his mind if he even made a move toward her. Somehow, that wasn't what he wanted—he had visions of her warm and willing in his arms.

"You're reading too much into the labels, if that's

what's bothering you,'' he told her. The startled look in her eyes told him he was right on target. "Since neither of the girls have a second parent around they're probably just pretending we're them.'' He glanced over at his daughter and back to Laura. "To be honest about it, when I was called home last week after my mother became ill, Beth wanted us to pretend I'd never have to go away again. That's when I realized how much she missed me.'' He sighed. "I guess it's fair to say I've hated myself ever since. I've decided to do something about it.''

Somberly, Tom gazed down at Laura's clenched hands and troubled eyes. He felt her fears as clearly as if they were his own, and that, somehow, they were tied up with himself and Beth.

He could have confronted her, asked her questions about her personal life that might explain her reaction. But they were questions he had no right to ask, and for once he left them unsaid.

Laura was deeply touched by his confession. She'd often played Let's Pretend with Carly, too. It was a harmless enough game and Carly seemed to enjoy it. It was too bad Tom's game with his daughter had brought him heartache instead of pleasure, but it seemed easy enough to solve. He had to change the job that took him from home, whatever it might be.

Solving what was bothering her wasn't as easy to dismiss. If only she could bring herself to believe that it was only a harmless game of pretend behind the children's drawings.

If only she could make herself believe there was no possible close connection between his daughter and hers.

Chapter Two

FERTILITY CLINIC SCANDAL

Unsuspecting Couples Victims of Alleged Unauthorized Use of Fertilized Eggs.

Tom couldn't believe his eyes. Sure, he'd heard the rumors going around INS circles that female immigrants were being smuggled into the country to harvest their eggs. But this morning's headlines hit even closer to home.

If the clinic had obtained eggs from the illegals, he reasoned, what could have prevented them from using fertilized eggs taken from some of the clinic's patients and using them to impregnate less fortunate clients? Nothing.

Was there more of a connection between his daughter and Carly Edwards than met the eye?

He reread the article carefully. It sounded as if, even with so many safeguards in place in the relatively new field of human fertilization, the Eden Clinic's methods had been unethical and downright fraudulent.

Of course, in his case, there was no doubt in his mind about Beth's biological mother. He had only to look at his daughter to see a miniature version of his ex-wife Jody, auburn hair and green eyes and all.

He and Jody had been married for six years. After three, she'd decided she was bored with her career and wanted to be a full-time wife and mother. He hadn't tried to dissuade her—what decent man would have? He sobered when he recalled the treatments they'd gone through before they'd eventually been blessed with the miracle that was Beth.

He'd wanted children from day one, but it had taken Jody time to make up her mind to be a mother. They'd tried for a time, but Jody hadn't been able to wait for nature to take its course. They'd taken test after test, treatment after treatment, before finally going through the in vitro process at the Eden Clinic. Jody had become pregnant and given birth to their daughter. He'd been thrilled at her birth. Too bad Jody hadn't been for long.

His thoughts swung to Carly Edwards and the astonishing resemblance she bore to his own daughter. Comparing the rumors surrounding the clinic to the newspaper article, it didn't take a wild stretch of his imagination to believe Carly could be living proof of a possible switch in one of Jody's fertilized eggs.

The problem now was to find a way to prove it.

Maybe he ought to search the clinic's records before he made a complete fool of himself. With the rumors flying around INS circles, surely he had a valid reason to check them out for DNA similarities.

Maybe he should come right out and ask Laura Edwards if her daughter had been the result of the in vitro process. And if she had, where? Unless he was mistaken, the process had taken place at the Eden Clinic, the same clinic where he and Jody had been patients.

But, even knowing as little as he did of Laura, after her behavior yesterday and her reaction today, he suspected he didn't have a chance she'd willingly tell him the truth.

LAURA READ the newspaper headlines and the accompanying story in a state of shocked disbelief.

The doctors at the clinic where she was employed as a data-record librarian were accused of stealing fertilized eggs from unsuspecting women and impregnating them in other patients!

Troubled at the disclosure, Laura thought back on the preceding weeks, the general air of tension in the clinic and the unusual number of official visitors.

So *that* was why the directors had been in closed-door meetings all last week. And why her immediate supervisor had been so short-tempered and distracted. It sounded as if the rumors she'd only half heard and now subconsciously feared had turned out to be true.

Her heart began to pound as she turned the page and read the rest of the article. It went on to say that the alleged misappropriated fertilized eggs had been implanted in other women or shipped to medical research laboratories without the donors' knowledge.

No wonder the sight of Beth Aldrich dancing with Carly in identical costumes as Sugar Plum fairies had disturbed her! Had she been an unsuspecting recipient of someone else's fertilized egg?

The subconscious fear that had been nagging at her

since the holiday presentation grew until she was torn by its possible implications—that Carly and Beth were somehow related.

With a sinking heart, Laura scanned the article for a second time, and then again.

As she read, she thought back to the two miscarriages she'd had during the ten years she and Carl had been married. And to the hormone treatments and artificial insemination procedures that had proved ineffective. The news that the miraculous in vitro procedure was now available at the Eden Clinic had turned out to be their last hope. Days of prayers had followed until she and Carl had received the welcome news she was finally pregnant. Eight and a half months later, and six weeks after the accident that had taken Carl from her, Carly had been born.

Again and again, she read the article and the alleged instances where the fertilized eggs were said to have been switched. The longer she read, the more uneasy she became. How could she not have known what was going on under her nose?

Icy fingers of fear ran up and down her spine.

She recalled having been told three of her eggs had been successfully fertilized and the embryos implanted in her womb. And that only one had taken hold. Now that she read the newspaper article, could she even believe the embryos had actually been her own?

Had she only been a surrogate mother?

She told herself she was looking for trouble, worrying over nothing. But there *was* the unavoidable truth: Carly resembled neither herself nor Carl—not at birth or even today. No one in their families had ever had auburn hair. In fact, she and her sister Dina had often joked about Carly being the proverbial "milkman's child."

The final paragraph in the article sprang out of the printed page.

The clinic's records believed to substantiate the alleged illegal activity had been impounded by the courts last night.

Now, if she'd wanted to, she couldn't even look through the detailed patient record disks for information that might have given her the answers she had to have for her own peace of mind.

Maybe it was just as well the records weren't available, she told herself over the pounding of her heart. She couldn't have borne it if the records had told another story—that Carly wasn't her biological child. Not when every beat of her mother's heart told her Carly *was* her daughter.

In the background, she could hear Carly talking about her new friend, Beth Aldrich.

Unbidden came the memory of the startled look on Tom Aldrich's face when he'd seen the girls side by side backstage. Had he suspected more than just an uncanny resemblance, a fluke of nature? Was Beth, too, a result of in vitro fertilization?

And, if so, once Tom read the articles, what would he do?

Laura stared at the newspaper article until the printed words blurred in front of her eyes.

Was the secure future she'd managed to carve out for herself and Carly after Carl had been killed not so secure after all? Had their lives turned in a new, terrifying direction?

BY THE TIME Tom came to pick up Beth from school on Monday afternoon, he'd decided that now was the time to speak to Laura Edwards about the similarity between the girls. Although he was willing to bet his INS badge she would try to take her daughter and run, he had to talk to her before she disappeared. With Christmas vacation only a week away, he had the sinking feeling it was now or maybe never.

He parked his car and strolled over to the school's vine-covered brick entrance. He was early, but he didn't want to take the chance of missing Laura.

The winds picked up and the temperature was dropping steadily. Overhead, the skies darkened and it looked as if it were about to rain. He shivered in his woolen jacket. In minutes, the odor of dust and moisture that heralded the approach of one of Los Angeles's infrequent fall rains filled the air.

The school bell rang. Children poured out of the large double doors.

He paced the walkway, searched the parking lot for Laura and checked his watch every few minutes. Laura Edwards *had* to arrive soon—she didn't seem to be the type to leave her kid waiting in a parking lot.

He wondered if she was being deliberately late so they'd wouldn't run into each other. If so, she had another think coming. Knowing what he knew about crimes that weren't reported in the newspapers, he wasn't about to leave Carly unattended. Any more than he would have left his own daughter.

Just as he spotted Beth and Carly skipping toward him, he caught sight of Laura getting out of a taxi.

"Where have you been?" he demanded as Laura rushed by calling out to Carly.

As she passed without stopping, she threw a startled look at him. Maybe she thought it was none of his business. Too bad. She didn't know it yet, but from now on he intended to make Carly Edwards and her mother his business.

"I got worried when you didn't show up," he said after he'd made his way through small groups of parents picking up their children and caught up with her.

"I had car trouble," she answered breathlessly over her shoulder. "Luckily, a cab came along or I wouldn't be here now." She opened her arms as her daughter came running. "But thank you for worrying about Carly. She would have waited for me."

"Not alone," he replied firmly. "And not while I'm around."

The frosty look she gave him was enough to put out the flame on a burning candle. "Carly and I have discussed this contingency," she replied over Carly's head. "She would have gone back into the building and waited for me in the school office. Right, sweetheart?"

Carly nodded.

"You should have called the school office so they could have kept her inside until you showed up," Tom admonished.

The closed look on Laura's face told him he was out of line. Maybe she was right, but he felt he had vested interest in Carly's safety. He decided not to belabor the subject, and certainly not in front of two interested little girls. And definitely not if he wanted to have Laura answer a few personal questions.

"Why don't you let me drive you and Carly home?" he offered, abruptly switching tactics.

The look in Laura's eyes turned wary. "No, thanks. The cab's waiting."

Tom nodded over his shoulder. "If you're referring to the cab that brought you, perhaps you'd better re-think that." The cab was gone. "Now, will you let me drive you?"

"I wouldn't want to put you out. I'll go inside and use the school's phone to call for help."

Tom mustered up his most inviting smile. "It looks as if it's about to rain. You wouldn't want to get caught in it, now, would you?"

The weather seemed to be a safe enough subject with Laura. Besides, he couldn't let her get away from him now. Not when he'd geared himself up to asking her the circumstances surrounding Carly's birth.

He told himself his only motive was to keep her with him as long as possible so he could ask her a few pertinent questions. But as he waited for her re-ply, he knew it was much more than that. He found himself lost in the intriguing hazel eyes that held the secrets he had to unlock. Then, too, there was the way the wind curled her chestnut hair around her upturned face, and the faint scent of lilacs that clung to her.

He began to realize how long it had been since he'd been attracted to one special woman—a woman like Laura. Not that he hadn't had his share of female companionship when he wanted it. After his divorce he'd even had a few relationships, but nothing lasting and none worth remembering.

But Laura Edwards was different. Although he'd only known her for a few short days, he'd found she was not only lovely, she was a beguiling combination of soft femininity and steel-like strength. There was an aura about her that turned a man's thoughts to the possibility of their becoming more than chance acquaintances.

Laura met his gaze. Surely, the steady look he was giving her was more than that of a Good Samaritan. It was the look of a man aware of her as a desirable woman.

Even while common sense told her to take him up on his offer, her warring senses told her to take care, to be on her guard, to beware of the glint in those golden-brown eyes.

Before she realized what was happening, she found herself responding to the pleasurable, warm sensations his gaze sent through her. Sensations she'd managed to put behind her six years ago.

In a way, she thought, it was reassuring to discover she was still woman enough to draw the gaze of a strong, virile, good-looking man like Tom Aldrich. At the same time, an inner voice told her he might turn out to be the last man in the world whose interest she should want to attract.

"Mommy, can we go with Beth and her daddy? Can we?"

Laura tore her thoughts away from Tom and tried to concentrate on Carly's question. With the newspaper headlines and the fear of losing her daughter not far from her mind, her first instinct was to refuse his offer—to stay as far away from him as possible. But there was Carly to consider.

It *was* cold, and steadily becoming colder. The skies were covered with billowing dark clouds that were fast obscuring the last rays of afternoon sunshine. She shivered as the clouds parted and there was the sound of thunder.

In the end, it was the yearning in Carly's voice and the arrival of the first drops of rain on her face that decided her.

Maybe she was being foolish in reading something into his gaze that might not be there. Anyway, there was no point in reading more into Tom's offer than normal courtesy.

"Thank you," she said, putting her fears aside. "We'll be glad for the ride home."

She saw a look of relief pass over his eyes before he nodded and turned to lead the way to his car. Relief? Why relief when all she was doing was accepting a ride home?

Laura became less sure she was doing the right thing. If the rain hadn't started in earnest, she would have been tempted to take Carly and go back into the school to call for a taxi.

"Seat belts, back here," Tom reminded the two girls as he unlocked the car doors and helped the children in. He held the car door open for her.

"Where to?"

"I live in the hills above Northridge," she answered and gave him directions. "I hope I'm not taking you out of your way."

"Not to worry. I did offer, you know," he said cheerfully.

"Yes, you did." Laura agreed. She took a deep breath. If the man had an ulterior motive, it was only going to be a matter of time before he gave himself away. She'd watch herself—forewarned was fore-armed.

"Nice area," he commented as he headed north across the valley to the hills. "Live there long?"

"Yes, over six years. We bought the house when we found I was expecting Carly."

"We?"

"My late husband, Carl, and I. We'd been renting, but decided living in a four-room apartment was no way to bring up a child. We had great plans for the baby. Unfortunately, my husband died before he had a chance to see his daughter," she added quietly.

"I'm sorry to hear that," he replied. "It must have been hard on you."

"Yes, it was, but time has a way of healing. Besides, Carl left me a part of himself in our daughter." She glanced out the car window and gestured to the pine trees and the low hills that appeared at the end of the street. "I'd always dreamed of living in the mountains, surrounded by trees and preferably near water," she said with a light laugh. "I'm afraid this is as close to my dream as I'll get."

"I like the mountains, too," Tom replied, determined to follow her lead and to keep the conversation cheerful. "In fact, I bought a cabin up in the San Bernardino mountains some years back—in Big Bear. There's enough trees up there to satisfy anyone and a small lake nearby. Small enough to freeze over in the winter."

"Sounds wonderful." Why was he telling her this, she wondered. "Do you get up there very often?"

He frowned at her question. "Not as often as I like."

"Because your work takes you away so much?"

"Partly," he answered, his smile fading fast. "My former wife decided she didn't like the mountains after all. That, and a few other things."

"Other things?"

"Marriage and motherhood, for a couple," he answered with a shrug of his shoulders. "The rest didn't matter, not to me, anyway."

"I'm sorry, I didn't mean to pry."

"You weren't. It's no secret Jody and I separated when Beth was a baby. We decided to make the split permanent over two years ago. I was awarded custody of Beth when the judge heard that Jody wasn't interested in motherhood after all."

"I can't imagine any woman changing her mind about becoming a mother," she said softly. "When I found I was finally able to have a baby after years of believing I'd never be able to have a child, I was overjoyed."

Tom nodded and stared off into the distant mountains. Laura's remarks suggested that Carly could have been an in vitro baby. The first piece of the puzzle fell into place. Now, he had to find out where and when.

"I felt the same way when we were finally able to have Beth," he agreed. "I haven't been around that much, but things are going to change soon. I'm going to be a real father from now on—especially since my mother isn't well and won't be able to take care of Beth for some time."

"I'm sorry to hear that," Laura answered. "Are you planning to be an at-home dad?"

"For a while." He grinned. "But, for Beth's sake, I've decided to look for reliable help."

Compassion for him stirred in Laura once again. In spite of his rugged exterior, Tom Aldrich was a man she could relate to. Life hadn't been all that easy for him, either. She had to remind herself not to feel sorry for him, not to care about him too much. She wasn't sure why she felt this way about him, but she sensed nothing could come of caring for him but heartache.

"We do what we have to do to survive, don't we?" she asked quietly.

He cast a quick glance at her before he nodded.

The quiet in the back seat finally registered. A quick glance over Laura's shoulder showed her both Carly and Beth were avidly listening to the conversation in the front seat and exchanging knowing glances.

Knowing glances? The two girls hadn't spoken a word since they'd gotten into the car. How could each know what the other one was thinking? What could there possibly be behind those knowing glances and secret smiles, she wondered.

"Here we are," she said as her home came into view. She pointed to a low, rustic house surrounded by a white picket fence. Its bright-yellow exterior shone like a candle through sheets of rain. A huge weeping willow tree graced the front yard. Under it, the flat of colorful pansies she'd started to plant was soaking up the rain.

"I wish I hadn't left the garage door opener in my car," Laura said as the rain drummed against the car's windshield. "We could have driven in out of the rain."

"That's okay," he answered. "If we move fast we won't get too wet."

"We?"

He grinned at her. "Yeah. Me and Beth. Frankly, I was hoping you'd invite us in for a hot drink."

Laura's stomach lurched, even as she nodded her agreement. He was being too friendly for comfort, but she couldn't turn him down. A favor deserved a reward, after all. Her mind moved swiftly, trying to decide what was behind Tom's continued interest.

"Cool! Can Beth and I have hot chocolate with marshmallows, Mommy?"

"Of course," Laura answered when it appeared Carly and Beth had heard every word she and Tom had exchanged.

"Come on, ladies," Tom said. "Let's see how fast we can make it out of the rain." He gathered the girls under his jacket and called back, "wait here for me, Laura. I'll come back for you as soon as I get the girls onto the porch."

She shook her head and started after the trio, smiling at the sight of Tom sheltering the girls from the rain with his jacket. He looked like a huge black bird, wings outstretched, ready to fly. "Hold on tight, or I'll fly away," she heard him call.

Beth's laughter sounded through the rain. "Daddy! You're silly!"

"Yeah," Carly echoed. "Everyone knows people can't fly without wings!"

"So what do you think these are?" he answered, flapping his arms. The girls giggled.

Laura reached the porch in time to see Beth snuggle close to her father. After a moment's hesitation,

Carly joined in the fun and, to Laura's surprise, snuggled up to him, too.

Laura dug in her purse for her keys. A warning bell went off in her mind at the sound of Carly's laughter, not that she needed to hear another warning. She was more certain than ever that Tom Aldrich had a motive for being here.

"Carly, why don't you and Beth take off your wet jackets and go dry your hair while I fix hot drinks?"

"Sure, Mommy," Carly answered happily. "I want to show Beth my dolls and my room, anyway."

Laura turned back to check out Tom. Soaking wet, he was in the process of taking off his wet jacket. The front of his sweater was wet with rain, and water trickled down the back of his neck. She felt guilty at having ignored him.

"You look a little worse for wear," she said. "There's another bathroom through that door, if you'd like to dry off."

She wasn't about to comment on how great he looked. Nor on the way his forest-green sweater clung to his broad chest and shoulders. When he ran his fingers through his damp hair and an errant lock of light-brown, wavy hair came to rest across his forehead, her fingers itched to brush it away from his clear, brown eyes.

"Thanks, I would." With an apologetic grin, he looked around the kitchen for a place to hang his wet jacket.

"Here, let me take that," she told him. When he handed her the jacket, his damp fingers brushed against hers. Like his gaze, his fingers sent a wave of warmth through her.

She sighed. How was she going to be able to keep her distance when the mere touch of his fingers or a simple glance sent waves of awareness of his masculine attraction through her?

When the door closed behind him, she breathed a sigh of relief. She hung the jacket in the small porch, grabbed a kitchen towel and dried off her own hair. The sooner she served the drinks, the sooner Tom would leave.

Laura was mixing cocoa with hot milk when he came back to join her. A plate of pumpkin-and-raisin cookies waited on the table. The aroma of freshly brewing coffee filled the kitchen.

"Can I do anything to help?"

"You can call the girls and tell them their hot chocolate is ready," she answered without looking at him. Wondering at her change in mood, Tom went to the door and called the girls. In spite of the warm and comforting scent of chocolate, it began to feel as if the cold wind blowing outside had found its way into the kitchen. Even the soft curtains that hung on the windows seemed to have stiffened with the cold.

What had he done to offend her now?

He couldn't keep up with Laura. One moment she was the smiling woman he'd admired, the next a cold block of ice. As soon as she'd thawed out so that she was at least approachable, she iced up again. Right now, her expression was strained, apprehensive.

If Beth hadn't been so happy to be here, he would have collected her and headed on home. Or, maybe he shouldn't have invited himself inside in the first place.

On the other hand, a lot rested on an important question he intended to ask.

The girls came running down the hall. "Daddy, Carly has a whole collection of Barbie dolls! Ken, too! She says I can come and play with them during Christmas vacation! Can I?"

"Come and drink your chocolate before it gets cold," Laura interjected before Tom could reply. A quick glance told him she'd interrupted him deliberately. Hell, he thought, if she wanted to get rid of him, she should have said so.

He glanced over at the girls who were busily picking out the tiny marshmallows floating on the surface of their drinks. The identical look of concentration on their faces and the similar way the tips of their tongues were caught between their teeth accentuated their striking look-alike appearance. Coupled with their damp auburn ringlets and green eyes, they could have been twins.

"Those two have to be related," he said impulsively. "Are you sure you're not one of my ex-wife's lost relations?"

Startled by the question, the girls paused openmouthed, their spoons in the air. Tiny marshmallows stuck to their lips.

"What did you say?"

They all jumped when the coffee cup Laura held in her hand fell to the floor and rivulets of coffee ran from the broken pieces. Her face was ashen, her voice tight.

Tom silently cursed the impulse that had blown the afternoon wide open—until he realized Laura's non-verbal response had told him everything he wanted to know.

Chapter Three

For a man who had successfully spent the last ten years working undercover and who should have known better, Tom had done the unforgivable: He'd let his mouth run away with him.

After seeing Laura's reaction to his impulsive comment about the possibility their daughters might be related, he'd made his exit with the few shreds of dignity he had left.

The brief exchange had left him more certain than ever that Laura also suspected Beth and Carly were related. And that his bringing his thoughts out into the open had scared the living daylights out of her.

Now he had to prove if he was right. Not that he had a clue where to start.

"Daddy, *why* couldn't I stay and play with Carly and her Barbie dolls?" Beth asked on the way home.

"I told you when we left, pumpkin," Tom said patiently, even though his mind was whirling with possibilities on how he could find the truth. "It may be the last week of school, but you still have homework to do. And Carly has hers, too. Besides, her mother still has to make dinner."

"Carly invited me to dinner," she persisted. "So why couldn't I stay?"

"Maybe Carly invited you, but her mother didn't," Tom replied. "It wouldn't have been polite to accept."

Laura hadn't invited him to dinner either, not that the lack of an invitation surprised him. Not after he'd opened his mouth and jumped with both feet into trouble. "Besides, we weren't expected. Maybe her mom wasn't prepared to feed all four of us." When he saw the disappointment on Beth's face, he tried to placate her. "I'm sure there'll be some other time when we'll be welcome."

He felt like a heel. He wasn't being honest with Beth and he knew it. After today, there probably wouldn't be "some other time," and they sure weren't going to be welcome. Good thing he was planning on their leaving for the mountain cabin as soon as school was out.

"Daddy, why—"

"Hold up a minute, pumpkin," Tom said as he maneuvered his way through a flooded intersection. The rain hadn't let up, and neither had the traffic. The trouble with rain was that it didn't happen often enough for most of Los Angeles's drivers to know how to cope with slick, wet streets, he thought sourly. He shifted to low gear and inched his way through the intersection. After narrowly avoiding a car that swerved too close for comfort, he unclenched his teeth. "Okay, pumpkin, you were asking…?"

"I wanted to know why Carly's mommy is mad at you."

"What makes you think she's mad at me?" Poor

kid, she would have had to have been deaf, dumb and blind not to have seen Laura's reaction to his impulsive question. She probably thought they'd gone mad.

"Well, because of the funny way she acted when you asked if we were related. She looked scared." Beth regarded him solemnly. "Daddy, why did you scare Carly's mother?"

So he hadn't been the only one to recognize Laura's shocked reaction was one of fear. He didn't have a sensible answer he could give Beth even if he wanted to. He *didn't* know why Laura had reacted the alarming way she had, but he sure intended to find out. He glanced over at Beth. She had a thoughtful look on her face as she waited for his reply. He had to call her off before she launched into a myriad of questions he wasn't able to answer. Not yet, anyway. He hated to lie to her, especially for something that was obviously important to her.

Beth rested her chin on one small hand and gazed up at him. "Are we related, Daddy?" Her trusting innocence shone from her clear, green eyes. The same eyes, he realized, she shared with Carly Edwards.

"I was only joking," he answered, reluctantly adding another fib to the long list of fibs he was fast accumulating.

He couldn't tell her what he was thinking. Certainly not now, and maybe never. At least, not until he could find the evidence that would bear out his gut feeling.

Even so, he was afraid it was a matter of time before the girls themselves began to wonder about their strong resemblance to each other. A matter of time before they started asking questions he and Laura would *have* to consider.

He breathed a sigh of relief when Beth accepted his answer without comment and turned her attention to the rain.

As far as he could see, he had to come up with some answers soon. Beth might only be turning six years old, but she was damn smart for her age. If Carly was anything like her, she had to be smart, too. Sooner or later they were bound to realize there had to be a reason why they were so much alike, sharing the same appearance, thoughts and mannerisms. So much so, they could have been twins, or at least, sisters.

Even Carly's mother must have thought so or she wouldn't have been so shocked at his remark.

After a moment's reflection, he realized that if he'd found himself in her position, especially after Sunday's newspaper headlines, the very idea that the kids could be related would have sent him as far away from him as possible. No one would have been able to take his Beth—unless it was over his dead body! He was sure Laura felt the same way about her daughter.

He couldn't let Laura and Carly disappear. He couldn't bear the idea that he may have found a child of his only to lose her.

He had to do something to prevent Laura from leaving, and fast.

THAT EVENING, Beth was watching her favorite television program and Tom was in the kitchen getting ready to pop a couple of frozen dinners into the mi-

crowave when the telephone rang. The unexpected
voice at the other end of the phone sent icy fingers
racing down his spine.

"Hi, Tom. It's Jody. I happened to be in town and
thought I'd touch base with you and see how things
are going."

His ex-wife's voice was syrupy sweet and an unwelcome sound out of his past, where he would have
been happy to leave her. Hell, he thought with a grimace, just the sound of her voice was enough to set
his nerves on a rampage.

His sixth sense told him Jody had surfaced for a
reason and it wasn't because she actually missed him
or their daughter. Jody hadn't been interested in how
things were going with either of them since their divorce, and he didn't think she was interested in him
now.

"Touch base, my eye!" he answered. "You
haven't picked up the phone to call to see how Beth
and I were doing in two years. What made you think
about us now?"

"Actually, it was Beth I wanted to know about,"
she replied, the syrup gone. "After all, I *am* her
mother."

"As far as I'm concerned, that was just an accident
of birth," he said. "You were never interested in her
or you wouldn't have left her the way you did. Hell,
you haven't even taken the time to call to check up
on her, either."

"You're wrong," she protested. "I *am* interested
in my daughter."

He laughed bitterly. "Lightning would have to
strike me first before I believed that. Come on, Jody,

you forget who you're talking to. *I'm* the guy who remembers you when.''

''People can change, you know,'' she answered defensively. ''Why can't you give me any credit for changing, too?''

He snorted. Memories of Jody's self-centered behavior were still all too vivid for him to buy she'd had a change of heart about being a mother. ''Maybe it's because I know you so well. You never cared about anything or anyone except yourself while we were married, and I don't believe you do now. So, tell me. What is it that you have your heart set on getting this time?''

''I want to see Beth.''

''Why now?'' he asked, alert to the lack of emotion in her voice. If she'd at least sounded as if she actually missed Beth, maybe he would have reconsidered. Without that signal, his instinctive reaction was to keep them as far apart as possible. ''Why now after two years?''

''I told you. I want to see Beth. The truth is, I've discovered I miss her.''

''Like hell you do. Think again.'' Tom figured that since he'd been awarded sole custody of Beth, he had nothing to lose by dealing straight with Jody.

Until a realization, as sharp as the bolt of lightning he'd mentioned, struck him. ''Been reading the newspapers lately?'' he asked. He knew the answer before she took the bait.

''Why, yes, I have. As a matter of fact, I find them very interesting. Don't you?''

He knew he'd found the real reason for Jody's unexpected telephone call. She'd read the headlines and had smelled a chance to get her hands on money. Not that she needed it. Their divorce settlement had practically wiped him out. All he'd kept was his daughter, the car and the house, with a hefty mortgage. At the time, he'd figured he'd come out ahead. He still did.

"Not particularly," he answered casually. "After all, the headlines don't involve me."

"And what if there *is* a chance they might involve us?"

"No way, Jody," he replied. "There's not a chance of anything having gone wrong when we were treated at Eden, and you know it. One look at Beth and you'd be laughed out of court. Providing you got that far."

"You're mistaken," she said. "So, are you going to let me see Beth or not?"

"No," he answered flatly when he realized the TV had been turned off. He had to end the conversation before Beth wandered into the kitchen looking for dinner. "If you really cared about Beth, you'd forget the whole thing."

"We'll have to see how right I am, won't we?" she returned in a voice back to dripping with sugar. "I'll call you again." Before he could reason with her, she hung up on him.

He might have known Jody wouldn't listen to reason. But one thing he did know, he had to find a way to keep her from upsetting Beth.

And, until he could prove to himself that Carly wasn't his and Jody's biological daughter, he had to keep Jody away from Carly, too. If Jody had the slightest inkling Carly's birth was the result of a switch of embryos, there'd be hell to pay. And Laura would be the one to make the payment. He already thought too much of her to let her be hurt.

ON TUESDAY, after he dropped Beth at school, Tom drove to the Eden Clinic. When he and Jody had been patients there, the parking lot had been full and the clinic's halls had teemed with hopeful patients. The walls were hung with framed letters from grateful parents; some had even generously contributed to the clinic's endowment fund. Gazing at the inactivity now, he wondered just who had been the beneficiaries of that fund.

Today, the lot was almost empty and although the halls were decorated for Christmas, they echoed with an eerie silence.

Once inside, Tom got as far as the blond receptionist. He blinked. In a low-cut red velvet dress that barely covered her ample endowments, she was dressed more for a dinner date than a day job.

He came to a halt in front of her desk and waited until she looked up from the magazine she was reading.

"What can I do for you?" she asked, her attention obviously still on the magazine.

Tom searched his memory for the name of the doctor who had been in charge of his and Jody's treatment. Thankfully, there was a directory over the receptionist's head. "Peterson, that's it. I'd like to see Dr. Peterson."

"I'm sorry," the bored woman replied. "Dr. Peterson is out of town."

"When do you expect him back?"

"I really can't say," she answered with a shrug of

her shoulders. Her long beaded red earrings jangled against her ruby lips and did a number on Tom's nerves in the bargain.

The last thing he wanted to do was to get into a verbal confrontation with someone who probably knew little about what was going on in the clinic and who cared even less.

"Can't or won't?" He tried to be polite, but her studied look of disinterest was getting to him, fast.

She shrugged again and reached for the ringing telephone. He waited impatiently while she repeated what seemed to be her stock reply. Not only was Peterson away, but it appeared so was the entire staff of doctors.

"You'll have to try back some other time," she said as she dropped the receiver into its slot. She glanced at her watch, reached for her purse, took out a compact and checked her appearance. For the first time since he'd walked in the door, she seemed to come to life. It was obvious that what he wanted—and what he wasn't going to get—was information on where to find the clinic's files.

The unusual quiet was broken when a flock of reporters and cameramen came noisily through the double glass doors. The receptionist perked up at the sight of the animated group and quickly forgot him. Now he knew why she'd been primping. The newspaper headlines had attracted media and press attention and she was ready for it.

Tom glanced at the directory on the wall behind her—there ought to be someone in the building who could help him. Or, failing that, someplace where he could find the information he needed.

The records room was 114, which according to a wall sign was around the corner. Good! With the receptionist's attention directed to the cameras, Tom disappeared from her sight.

Even though the newspaper had indicated the clinic's records had been impounded and sealed, that wasn't going to stop him. Armed with his official INS badge and the rumors circulating throughout the Service, he was pretty sure he had enough grounds to brazen his way into the files. Better yet, if the clerk in charge of the clinic's records was anything like the receptionist, maybe he could send her outside to share in the spotlight.

The heavy door opened easily under his hand. Sure enough, there was a clerk standing behind the counter, her back to the door as she filed manila folders in the walled bookcase. The sight of her familiar, slender figure stopped him in his tracks. His studied smile faded when she started to turn around.

The clerk was Laura Edwards!

Seldom at a loss for words, his request for access to patient records froze in his throat. Of all the women in the world, how could he be so unlucky to have drawn the one woman who was the most likely to refuse to listen to him?

''Can I help…? Her voice trailed off as she faced him. Judging from her reaction, she might have seen the devil. Her face paled, her fingers covered her lips. He felt terrible.

Why was it, he wondered, that every time he managed to upset Laura Edwards, he wanted to take her in his arms? Not only to ask for forgiveness for whatever it was he might have done, but to bask in the warmth of her soft femininity. To draw in the unique scent that clung to her and to taste her kissable lips. The temptation lingered even though he knew his gut reaction was out of place and, definitely, ill-timed.

"This is a surprise!" he exclaimed with a forced smile. "You're the last person I had expected to find here. Why didn't you tell me you worked at the clinic?"

"You didn't ask," she answered, obviously as shocked by their encounter as he was. "What are you doing here?"

From the look on her face, he knew he didn't have to explain. Certainly not after his outburst yesterday. He knew by now Laura was no fool; she had to share his suspicions.

Now that he'd gotten this far, he was determined to find out how long she'd worked here at the clinic. And to find out if she'd been a patient at the clinic the same time that he and Jody were being treated. If she had, surely she must have put one and one together and checked the clinic's records for herself by now.

He could see Laura's fingers tremble on the folders she was holding. Her lips tightened as their gazes locked.

One thing was obvious from her reaction, he wasn't going to be able to charm his way into the clinic's records now.

"You just might help me, at that," he finally answered cheerfully. "I'd like to look at a couple of files."

"No!" she said quickly, too quickly. "That is," she added as she made a visible attempt to pull herself together, ''the clinic's records aren't open to the public.''

''I wouldn't say I was exactly the public,'' he answered. He started to reach for his INS badge, when he was struck by her genuine distress. He was about to ask what she had to lose by allowing him to view the records, when he realized that if what he suspected was true, she might in fact have a lot to lose.

''Surely you must know the records have been impounded and sealed by the courts,'' she continued. She glanced over her shoulder and just as quickly glanced away. ''There's no way you, or anyone else for that matter, can view them.''

She hadn't moved fast enough. His gaze followed hers to a door marked Private and sealed with official yellow tape. Now, if he could only persuade her to let him get in there long enough to check for DNA results in his file and in hers.

''Not even you?''

''Not even me,'' she answered. ''Besides, all the old records have been destroyed. Now they only exist on CD ROMs.''

''How do you know which records I'm interested in, or that they're old ones?'' he asked. When she flushed, he knew he had her. There was a saying around the Service that if you kept a suspect talking long enough, he'd trip himself up. Laura was no different than anyone else who had something to hide.

She met his gaze squarely, but the color hadn't come back into her face. She still looked as if she'd seen the devil. Her figure tensed and her eyes darted to the door behind him as if she were ready to run.

Tom marveled at the change in her in the short

space of three days. She may have been a vision in a dark-blue pant suit, with a pale-yellow T-shirt that showed under her open jacket, but there were deep shadows under her hazel eyes.

She was definitely not the happy, smiling woman who had attracted his attention at the Beckwith Day School recital last Friday.

He forced himself to dismiss the thought that he would have liked to take her in his arms. To tell her that everything was going to be all right. He couldn't, not when he was the reason for her distress. And not until he could be sure his suspicions were wrong.

Unless he missed his guess, if Laura had gone through the in vitro process she had to have viewed her records some time or another. Since she had the clinic's records at her fingertips, curiosity alone would have made her do it. If he'd been in her position, he sure as hell would have done it.

"How about before the records were sealed?" he joked, not willing to give up without another attempt to persuade her to let him look at his file. "Were they available for viewing then?"

"Not even then," she replied. "All the clinic's employees are required to sign an agreement to honor patient confidentiality. The clinic operates on the honor system."

"Honor system?" he said dryly. "That's a peculiar way to describe a clinic accused of operating outside the law."

"Accused," she retorted. "It still has to be proved."

"It will, Laura. Mark my words, it will," he returned with a grim smile. "And when it is, I intend to be back."

Laura returned the gaze that drew her like a magnet. She was afraid that behind that smile he was able to see into her mind, to sense her thoughts, to hear the pounding of her heart. Apprehension rose through her until she could taste her fears.

How far had that appealing smile of his taken him in the past and where did he expect it to take him now?

If he thought she could be persuaded to cut the official tape that sealed the room where the computer disks were stored, he had the wrong woman, she told herself resolutely. He must know she had too much to lose by putting herself and her job in jeopardy. She didn't intend to be manipulated by his smile or anything else he had in mind.

She should have sent him on his way before now, but some emotion deep inside her responded to the way he looked at her. She forced herself to face a truth she'd been trying to ignore. Tom Aldrich and his sheer aura of innate masculinity had awakened feelings in her she'd spent six years trying to forget.

He made her realize how much she missed being held in a man's arms, feeling his solid male strength against her. Running her hands over warm, bare skin, to twine her fingers in his hair. Sharing his embraces. And not just with any man, but with Tom Aldrich.

Since Carl, she hadn't met another man who managed to stir her dormant sensuality the way Tom had managed to do.

But what good would it have been to lose herself

in the dream of swimming in a sea of sensuality with Tom's arms around her when he was a threat to her?

She couldn't allow herself to think about him like this, she told herself. She couldn't allow herself to feel again, and if she had an ounce of brains in her head, certainly not with him.

Now that she'd put the newspaper headlines together with her subconscious fears, she sensed Tom Aldrich was too dangerous a man to care for. There was a clear line drawn between them that neither could afford to cross. Until that line was erased, and she could be sure no one could take Carly from her, the attraction she and Tom obviously felt for each other was hopeless.

"I'm sorry," she told him. "My answer is still the same. No one is allowed into the files."

His smile faded from his eyes, but not from his lips. With a nod, he saluted her, turned on his heel and left.

Laura collapsed into a chair. If she'd been trying to convince herself that Carly and Beth Aldrich couldn't possibly be related, Tom's unexpected appearance had told her otherwise. Either he knew something she didn't, or he was bluffing. Either way, he spelled trouble. She told herself she still had no reason to believe he was after records involving Carly's birth. She had to believe that the amazing similarities between Carly and Beth were pure chance.

As for her being allowed to read the clinic's records, she'd told him the truth. Sure, after the possibility that the girls were somehow related had begun to dawn on her, she had been on the verge of coming to the clinic to find her file. And, after Tom's outburst, she'd even considered looking into his. She might have, except when she'd come to work this morning, she'd found the door to the files had been taped closed. Short of drawing attention to herself, she had to live with the rules.

She gazed at the sealed door. There was no use in torturing herself with possibilities or with Tom's motives for showing up at the clinic this morning. The window of opportunity to search the records had closed.

Chapter Four

"It's not over until it's over," Tom told himself as he drove to his office at the Federal Building in downtown Los Angeles. There was still the strong possibility that Carly Edwards could be his daughter. Or, at the very least, if one of Jody's eggs had been fertilized by Carl Edwards's sperm, that the child was Beth's half sister. Either way, it wasn't a possibility he was prepared to ignore.

"It takes real dedication for a guy to come in to work when he's on emergency family leave." His partner Len Orstan laughed when Tom showed up in the office they shared. "Leisure time too much for you to handle?"

"Hell, no," Tom muttered. "I haven't had any downtime yet to enjoy. As a matter of fact, I'm busier now than ever. I came to ask you for a favor."

"Make it something that doesn't take any physical or mental effort." Len popped an antacid pill in his mouth, downed it with water and groaned. "I'm still suffering from a reaction to something I had for dinner last night. I don't know which feels worse, my head or my stomach."

"Maybe if you didn't eat those spicy concoctions you're so fond of, you wouldn't get indigestion so often," Tom commented as he enviously regarded his tall and lean partner. While he had to watch his own weight, the guy hadn't gained a pound in the ten years he'd known him.

"Hell, Tom," Len groaned, gingerly shifting in his seat, "you know I can't help myself. I have to keep my Kate happy. She keeps taking cooking lessons and coming up with new recipes for me to try."

"Why don't you have my mother give Kate some of her old-fashioned country cooking recipes?"

"I wish." Len gazed at the bottle of antacid pills on his desk and grimaced. "By the way, how is your mother?"

"She's doing okay, but she's going to be in a convalescent home for a while." Tom settled into a chair. "The doctors said she had a mild stroke brought on by too much activity. They could be right. I've already found taking care of an energetic kid is a full-time job. Not to mention the cooking, such as it is, trying to keep the house from falling down over my ears and answering the zillion questions Beth asks. I swear, it's enough to exhaust a saint. I'm going to have to find full-time help before I come back to work."

"And what if you don't find anyone?"

Tom shrugged. "I will. I have to."

"Maybe you can advertise for a mother's helper like Kate did. She found a college student who wants to work a few hours a day. Works out great for all of us."

"*Mother's* helper?" Tom felt affronted.

"Sorry, maybe I should have said Dad's helper." Len laughed at Tom's grimace. "Shouldn't be a problem." Len straightened abruptly and stared at Tom. "Say, you're not thinking of becoming a stay-at-home dad, are you?"

"No way!" Tom protested. He dropped into the chair behind the desk he occupied when he wasn't in the field. "You know, I realize now I didn't appreciate the help Mom gave me. I'm going to have to make it up to her somehow." He rubbed the back of his neck in his frustration. "In the meantime, I'll have to hire someone to help out after the first of the year—after we get back from the mountains."

"Good luck. So, what brings you here today?"

"Plenty," Tom answered. "Do you recall the rumors floating around the Service about a local clinic suspected of importing illegal females to harvest their eggs?"

"Sort of," Len replied after a moment's thought. "Actually, I haven't paid too much attention. But I did hear Manny Sorteze is looking into it, poor guy. It must be one hell of an assignment." He paused, made a face and rubbed his stomach. "It sounds like a crazy idea, but I guess it sure beats smuggling drugs. It may not be as lucrative, but if they get busted, the penalties are a hell of a lot less. Why do you ask?"

Tom leaned forward in his chair and lowered his voice.

"This is just between us, okay?"

"Okay." Len downed another pill, shuddered and sat back. "Sounds serious."

"It is," Tom assured him. "But the main point is

that what I'm about to tell you affects several lives. For starters, my daughters'."

A look of alarm passed over Len's face.

"Something wrong with Beth?"

"No. This is about the other one."

"The other one!" Len grinned broadly and slapped his knee. "Son of a gun! Who would have thought you're the kind of guy to have kids popping up all over the map?"

Tom frowned before he answered. "I'm not. You ought to know me better than that. I didn't even know this child existed until last week."

"No!" Len forgot his stomach and stared at Tom. "You mean her mother didn't tell you she was pregnant until now?"

"If you'll shut up for a minute and get your mind out of the gutter, I'll tell the whole story," Tom protested wearily. "But it's not for publication, understand?"

"Okay, but I'd still like to know how in the hell you become a father without knowing it."

"Simple. I suppose you've heard about in vitro fertilization?" Len nodded. "Well, it's no secret that Jody and I went to the Eden Clinic in order to conceive Beth."

"Say, isn't that the clinic you mentioned a minute ago? The one that made the newspaper headlines last Sunday?"

"Yes." Tom went on to tell Len about what had taken place in the past few days. He ended by telling him about his visit to the clinic that morning. What he didn't tell Len was the way he felt about Carly's mother. That part of the story was still too private to share.

Len sat speechless, the glass of water suspended in his hand. "You've got to be kidding!"

"Nope. Now, that's where you come in. Do you suppose you can get into those records and look up a few DNA results?"

"Now you're suggesting something highly irregular, maybe even illegal," Len finally replied. "At least, as long as the records are sealed by the courts."

"Not if you use the rumors running around here as a legitimate excuse to do some research for the Service."

Len gazed thoughtfully at the glass he held in his hand. "It might work, but I'd still have to get a court order, you know. And Manny might not like my interfering in his assignment."

"Yeah, I know. I'd ask Manny myself, but with my mother out of the picture, I've got Beth to take care of. And school vacation starts next week." Tom moved to the edge of his chair and spoke in an undertone. More depended on getting Len to help him than he knew. "There must be some judge who cooperates with the Agency."

"Maybe." Len shook his head. "Take my advice and stay out of it, Tom. If anyone found out about you and Jody having been patients of the clinic, it might be construed as a conflict of interest. There'd be hell to pay around here."

"There's going to be hell to pay if I don't do something now," Tom answered, remembering Jody's threats. "At least I'd have a head start."

"A head start in what?"

"Staying ahead of that ex-wife of mine. I have a hunch she's up to no good."

Len nodded. "Okay. Give me a few weeks. I'll talk to Manny and see what I can do. I'll let you know."

Tom stood and clasped his hand. "I want you to know it's more than a matter of curiosity for me, Len. Strangely enough, I've already begun to feel there's some kind of a bond growing between Carly Edwards and myself. Beth has bonded with her, too. Not that that's surprising—they're as alike as two peas in a pod."

"You don't say!"

"More than you know. But the bottom line is, since the kid doesn't have a father to watch over her, I feel responsible for her." He left out his concern for Laura and his growing interest in her.

Len nodded sympathetically. "I know all about fatherhood and what it can do to a man. Tell you what… I'll get back to you as soon as I can find a way to help you without causing an uproar. In the meantime, keep the faith."

Back in the car to pick up Beth from school, Tom pondered his next move. While Len tried to persuade Manny to delve into the clinic's records and get some answers, *he* was going to have to find a way to keep Laura from taking Carly and running.

As he drove off, he knew it was going to take more than an act of faith on his part to keep Laura and her daughter in his sight. But, come hell or high water, and whatever it took, keeping her in sight was exactly what he intended to do.

"DADDY! DADDY!"

Followed by Carly, Beth came running across the

school lawn to Tom. She skidded to a stop and threw herself into his arms. "Guess what! Carly's birthday is almost the same day as mine!"

"No kidding," Tom replied as soon as he could breathe again. He glanced over Beth's shoulder just as Laura joined them. "Looks as if we have ourselves a pair of Christmas babies."

"Almost," she answered—reluctantly, he thought. What was there about the girls having birthdays so close to each other that bothered her?

"Almost?"

"Actually," she explained, "Carly was born Christmas Eve."

"Close enough," he said with a speculative eye on the girls. "Beth was born Christmas morning."

"Yeah, Daddy says I was his Christmas present!" Beth paused for a moment and came up with another question. "Did you really find me under the Christmas tree, Daddy?"

"Sure, I did," he answered. "All wrapped in a big bright-red ribbon."

"Oh, Daddy!" Beth giggled. "You're being silly again!"

"It's because of that silly monster," he answered gravely. Beth blamed everything that went wrong on a make-believe monster. It was a game he'd discovered she liked to play, and he got a kick out of playing it with her.

His answer sent Beth and Carly into a fresh attack of giggles. Even Laura's serious gaze turned into a reluctant smile.

He winked and smiled back.

He liked seeing Laura smile. Tiny points of light lit up her incredible hazel eyes; the dimple in her right cheek moved in an enchanting waltz. And her lips! When they curved in a genuine smile, as they did now, they made an otherwise dreary day shine.

He glanced up at the sky. Sure enough, even as the thought came to him, a few rays of sunshine had managed to filter through the gathering clouds.

Considering the unfortunate way he and Laura had parted yesterday, he didn't feel now was the time to tell her how much he liked her smile.

"And, Daddy," Beth continued happily, "since I'm not going to have a birthday party of my own this year, Carly says I can come to hers!"

When Tom saw a look of surprise pass over Laura's face, a feeling of guilt swept over him. Maybe it *was* criminal not to give an almost-six-year-old girl a birthday party for her friends. If so, he was guilty. But somehow he didn't want Laura to think any less of him than she already did.

"I know it sounds like a lame excuse," he explained, "but I've been away from home so often in the past four years, my mother has been doing the birthday party planning. She's getting over an illness right now and hasn't had a chance to take care of a party this year." When the look of surprise became a question, he added, "With so much going on, I thought we'd just celebrate Beth's birthday privately."

He could read the question in Laura's eyes as clearly as if she'd spoken out loud. How could he not realize a kid wanted a party with her friends?

She was right. If he were any kind of a father, he'd

have seen to it Beth had some kind of birthday celebration planned in spite of his mother's illness.
Omissions such as this was one of the reasons he'd
made himself a promise to be a better father.

"Beth is welcome to share Carly's birthday party
this year, if you don't know how to plan one for her,"
Laura said. The tone of her voice and its unspoken
censure got to him.

"Mommy will teach you how, if you want," Carly
volunteered.

The last thing Tom wanted from Laura was a
teacher-pupil relationship. Even with the tension he
felt simmering beneath her smile, he had a wish for
something more. More of a man-woman thing, he
mused as he studied Laura, her skin glowing from the
winter wind. And definitely more than a mere friendship.

"Thanks," he said dryly, firmly putting aside his
sensual thoughts for the immediate problem of a little
girl's birthday celebration.

He made a mental note to ask Len about kids'
birthday parties. After all, the guy ought to be a vet-
eran party planner. He had five kids of his own.

"So when's the party?"

"This Saturday," Laura replied. "Since school
will be out for the winter break Friday, we're having
the party early. A number of Carly's friends are going
away on vacation and won't be available later." She
smiled ruefully. "We have this problem every year,
but at least this way her birthday doesn't get lost in
the Christmas celebration."

"As a matter of fact, we'll be leaving for the holidays, ourselves," Tom said. "Before my mother be-

came ill, I'd planned to have the family spend the holiday at my cabin up in Big Bear. Since Mom's going to be in a convalescent home for a time, she's told me to go ahead without her.''

A look of concern wrinkled Laura's forehead. ''I hope there's nothing seriously wrong with your mother.''

Tom added ''a caring woman'' to the growing list of attributes he liked about Laura. The list was growing fast.

''Not according to the doctors, thank goodness—it was a mild stroke. She's going to be just fine with some rest. I wish I'd taken the time to realize it's been a couple of rough years for her.''

''Couldn't your wife—''

''My *ex-wife*,'' Tom interrupted. ''I couldn't have asked her to help out, not after all this time, not that she'd be willing. Anyway, her career seemed to be more important than we were, and I doubt things have changed.''

He thought of Jody and the heartless way she'd left Beth's care to him and his mother. Jody and Laura were poles apart, he thought as he gazed at Laura. Where Jody lacked a mother's instinct, Laura appeared to be as loving a mother as any child could wish for. Too bad he couldn't say the same about Jody.

By the same token, he was guilty, too. He should have known that the full-time care of a lively little girl like Beth would be too much for his mother.

''Daddy,'' Beth spoke up, ''can Carly come up to the mountains with us?''

"No!" Laura said hurriedly, with panic in her voice. "We couldn't possibly."

Tom bit his lip at Beth's question. His daughter was cute, candid and full of childish enthusiasm, but she had this habit of speaking before she stopped to think. Still, he had to be honest. Beth's interruption was nothing compared to his own outburst yesterday.

He stared at Laura, suddenly at a loss for a reply to Beth's question. An invitation to a birthday party was one thing, but an invitation to a mountain cabin for the Christmas and New Year holidays was another. Not that he wouldn't have liked having Laura to share the holidays with them, but having her in close quarters when he couldn't touch her would sure as hell be enough to drive him crazy.

Considering how Laura tried to keep her distance, there wasn't a prayer for a pleasant, if not romantic, holiday anyway. How was he going to get out of this mess gracefully without looking like an ingrate?

Maybe he ought to talk about the mountain weather and the possibility of getting snowed in. Weather was safe. With the temperature dropping steadily every day along with the rain, there would be a white Christmas in the mountains for sure.

Visions of white snow piled high against the windows of his rustic cabin, a fireplace aglow with a comforting fire, and Laura in his arms flashed in front of his eyes. Soft music would be playing in the background, the children would be asleep in their beds, and the silver-and-gold ornaments on a Christmas tree he cut himself would reflect the fire's glow. Two forgotten wineglasses would be waiting on the low coffee table. He and Laura would exchange a lingering kiss under the mistletoe that hung above their heads. And then...

He caught himself before he pictured a scene that could arouse and embarrass him. Just the thought of it was enough to make a man agree to anything if he thought it was possible to make it come true. At the moment, though, it didn't seem possible at all. Not with the alarmed look growing in Laura's eyes.

It was a crazy vision, anyway. How could he be so interested in a woman he wasn't sure he could trust and who was wary of him? He had to change the subject away from the mountain cabin to something less worrisome. But first, there was Carly's birthday invitation to settle.

"Why don't we settle the birthday party before we make any future plans?" he said with an inward sigh. "Name the time and the place, and I'll have Beth there," he said.

"We're having the party at the Children's Corner in Sherman Oaks on Saturday, from two to four in the afternoon," Laura answered. Almost as if she were amused at some inner thought that had suddenly occurred to her, her eyes began to sparkle and a fresh smile curved at the corner of her lips. "You might want to turn the invitation down," she added with a grin. "I'm afraid this type of party might be an unusual experience for a man."

Tom wasn't about to give up now. Not when Beth appeared ready for tears. "How about for a guy who's trying to be a good father?"

She glanced down at Beth. A softer look passed over her face. "That might be a different story. That is, if you're really serious about learning how to put on birthday parties.''

''I am,'' Tom answered and raised his right hand. ''I swear I am, and I figure this just might be the time for a lesson. I don't expect to be caught short next year.''

''All right,'' she answered with a reassuring smile at Beth. ''You're invited.''

A weight seemed to fall off his shoulders.

''So, tell me, what's different about this party?''

''Everyone is supposed to bring their favorite doll, 'cause we're having a doll's tea party,'' Carly explained excitedly. ''And we have to get real dressed up for it!''

Tom thought about that for a moment. ''Dressed up in what?''

''In our mommies' shoes and fancy dresses. It's going to be a lot of fun!''

Tom swallowed hard at Beth's squeal of pleasure. If it was going to be a dress-up party in adult clothing, he had to come up with a costume for Beth in a hurry. His mother's shoes and dresses were out of the question. Maybe a visit to the nearest second-hand dress store would do the trick. As for him, he wondered, what did a grown-up man wear to a doll's tea party?

He felt Laura's eyes on him. ''Is there a problem?'' she mouthed. His bewildered thoughts busy trying to figure out a solution to the dress-up problem, he could only shrug and shake his head.

He envisioned himself at the doll's tea party—the only man in a group of little girls dressed up to look like miniature adults. He shuddered.

Realizing that Beth didn't have a mother at home,

Laura felt she would have had to have a heart of stone not to respond to the helpless look that came into Tom's eyes at Carly's description of the doll's tea party.

"Why don't you come up to my place so Beth can choose what she wants to wear from my closet?" Laura said impulsively. "Carly will be happy to help her."

"Sure," he agreed with a look of gratitude, "but what do I wear?"

"Same as usual," she answered, smothering a smile. With his very masculine looks Tom Aldrich was definitely a man's man. There was no way she could imagine him as a participant at the party. The tables were too short, the cups and saucers too small for a man built to his proportions. She felt herself blush at the thought.

"You can watch the action and learn about little girls' parties from the sidelines," she said. "Or," she added taking pity on him, "you can leave Beth with me on Friday. She can stay overnight and be ready for the party. You don't have to come, if you're uncomfortable with the idea."

"Please, Daddy! Can I?"

"Say yes, Mr. Aldrich!" Carly exclaimed. When she saw the look on her mother's face, she added, "Please."

After seeing the excitement on the children's faces, Tom knew he didn't have the heart to say no. "Are you sure?" he asked.

Laura nodded. She could see Tom's anxious expression turn to one of relief.

She stilled the small voice that warned her she was

letting her emotions get in the way of thinking clearly. She was allowing herself to care too much about this man and his too male appeal. Even as she fought the growing attraction between them, she knew he was a man to stay clear of.

That same small warning voice that had plagued her since she'd fallen into his arms reminded her that softening toward him was a sure way to court trouble. If she had the sense she was born with, she'd run, not walk, as far away from him as she could get before it was too late.

It was the happy smile on Beth's face that finally decided her to go through with the invitation to spend the night. She wasn't making the offer for Tom's sake, she told herself as she forced herself to return his grateful gaze. She was doing it for Beth, a small motherless child.

AFTER HE WATCHED Beth disappear through the school doors Friday morning, Tom glanced at his watch. Laura was late again. Considering her friendly offer to lend Beth one of her dresses for the tea party and to stay overnight, he'd expected to see her this morning so he could tell her how much he appreciated her offer.

Was she avoiding him?

He shook off the thought. After all, she'd seemed friendly enough the other day, or he wouldn't have agreed to let Beth stay overnight with her and Carly.

He was more than aware of Laura as a desirable woman, a lost cause if he ever heard of one. But he couldn't put aside the suspicion that she must have known something about the clinic's practices before they made the newspaper headlines and was hiding it from him.

All the more reason to keep an eye on her.

He decided to head home to get his thoughts in order and to start packing for the trip to the mountains.

It wasn't that he didn't feel bad for Laura and her heartbreak if it turned out Carly wasn't her biological child. He did. But there was a time when a guy had to think about himself, too.

How could a man not want to know his own child?

Chapter Five

The last person Tom wanted to see making herself at home in his kitchen was his ex-wife. After her telephone call, he might have known she'd show up. His euphoria faded faster than a blink of his eye.

By the time Jody had said goodbye two years ago, he'd been fed up with hearing her complaints about the draining demands of motherhood and her lost career. After years of no-win arguments, he hadn't been sorry to see her leave.

If it hadn't been for their daughter, he wouldn't have wasted his time thinking about her mother. Their last meeting in court had cured him of that.

It had been that meeting that had left him wanting nothing more to do with Jody. She'd shrugged her shoulders and mentioned the demands of her career when the judge had asked if she was certain she didn't want to share her daughter's custody. The look of disdain the judge had given her and the look of sympathy he'd given him had spoken louder than the terms of the final divorce decree giving him full custody of Beth. They'd both known Jody was a sorry excuse for a mother.

Until recently, Jody's track record had made him leery of career-minded women. Sure, it must be difficult to mix marriage, motherhood and career, but Laura's loving attitude toward Carly, and even his own Beth, had made him realize it was possible. Jody was in a class by herself.

Now here she was, smiling at him as though they'd parted amicably only yesterday.

All his senses snapped to alert at the smile he knew only too well was false. "What are you doing here?" he asked warily.

"Making myself a cup of coffee," Jody answered with a casual flip of her hand at the automatic coffeemaker. When his look registered, her smile faded. "You needn't look at me that way," she protested. "After all, this *was* my home."

"Was is right," he answered. "It stopped being your home two years ago when you asked for a divorce, packed up and left for good. Or don't you remember saying goodbye?"

"Oh, come on, Tom," she answered as she poured a cup of coffee. She offered it to him, but he waved it away. "I am Beth's mother. I never said I wouldn't want to visit her occasionally."

"As far as I was concerned, you stopped being Beth's mother at the time of our divorce," he retorted, pacing the kitchen floor. The dark-green squares in the linoleum echoed his mood. "Except for that phone call yesterday, you've never indicated an interest in visiting until now."

Her shrug angered him, but he knew he had to keep his cool if he was going to find out what she was up to.

"So, what made you change your mind now?"

She glanced over his shoulder without answering. "Where's Beth?"

"She's at a sleepover." At least Jody hadn't shown up when Beth was at home, he thought. He wouldn't have wanted her to think her mother had come home to stay. The kid's heart would only be crushed when Jody decided she'd had enough of motherhood, or accomplished whatever it was she'd come for.

Fighting to control his temper, he stopped in front of her. "You haven't answered me. I still want to know what fool notion brought you here this afternoon."

Jody casually walked around him to the refrigerator, took out a carton of cream and added some to her cup of coffee.

"Well?"

"I guess you could say I missed Beth."

"I *could* say that, but I'd only be kidding both of us," Tom replied. He had to fight the impulse to order her out of the house immediately; he had to know what she had on her mind so he could stay one step ahead of her. "I was your husband, remember? I know you too well. Beth had a rough time after you left, and I don't want you breaking the poor kid's heart again."

The thought occurred to him that while *he* might not want Jody around, maybe he owed it to Beth to allow her mother to stay and visit with her. But Beth wasn't around to ask, thank God. Frustrated at his mixed emotions, he thrust his balled fists into his pockets.

His gaze swept his ex-wife, mentally comparing

her to Laura. As far as he was concerned, there was nothing there to compare. Laura was all woman, tender and loving, concerned more with her daughter's happiness than her own. Jody was a self-centered woman, masquerading as a mother.

She was here for a reason, and it wasn't because she'd missed Beth. And not because she missed him, either.

"You'll have to wait until tomorrow," he said after reluctantly deciding maybe Beth's wishes were more important than his own distrust of Jody. Maybe a mother was a mother, even one like Jody.

He blamed himself for being softhearted and leaving the picture of the three of them in Beth's room. He'd hoped Beth would only remember the good times. Hopefully, Beth had been too young to remember the bad ones.

He tried a different tack. "How about if I bring Beth to visit you wherever you're staying?"

"Oh, that's not a problem," she answered with a bright smile. "I thought I'd spend a few days here with you and Beth."

Tom glanced around the room. It was then he noticed a small suitcase that had been deposited on a chair.

"I don't think so," he retorted. Who needed to go through hell twice? "I don't want to upset Beth if she finds you here unexpectedly. Why don't you get yourself a hotel and let me know where you are. If Beth wants to see you, I'll bring her over."

"A visit isn't exactly what I had in mind." Jody's clear green eyes, the color of Beth's, measured him over the rim of her coffee cup. Only where Beth's were the innocent eyes of a child, her mother's were hard and calculating.

Tom realized he wasn't going to get rid of Jody that easily.

"Exactly what did you have in mind?" His mind whirled with possibilities, but he couldn't come up with a damn thing that made sense other than Jody's possible interest in the Eden Clinic fiasco. One thing he was pretty sure of, Jody hadn't changed. "You washed your hands of Beth two years ago and you're not going to get them on her now."

"What makes you think Beth is the only one I'm interested in?"

Her gaze was meant to be coy, but he wasn't buying. He'd been fooled by that sultry invitation too many times before. If she thought she could soften him up in bed to get her way, she was mistaken.

He fixed her with a cold stare and laughed bitterly. "If you mean me, you can forget it."

He'd never meant anything so surely before in his life. No way was he going to go through the misery of reconciling with Jody. More to the point, he wasn't going to let Beth be hurt again.

He hadn't been interested in reconciling with Jody before and he wasn't now. And definitely not after he'd met a real woman like Laura Edwards.

Laura was the homespun type—open and caring, interesting to know and lovely to look at. Jody was more like an elegant cake covered with too much icing. When the icing came off, there wasn't a damn thing worthwhile underneath.

"So, do you need a ride to a hotel?" he asked. "I'll call a taxi."

"No, thanks," she answered. She poured herself another cup of coffee and settled down at the kitchen table. "It's still early. We need to talk."

Tom fixed her with the stare that had intimidated more than one guilty individual. "What is there to talk about now? We did enough talking two years ago."

"Us."

"I told you, there is no 'us,'" Tom said wearily. "There hasn't been for a long time. And that includes Beth, in case you need to be told."

She smiled. Tom remembered that vague, fake smile—it meant she hadn't listened to a word he'd said. She'd used it too many times in the past to placate him while her mind had been elsewhere. Usually on something she wanted. The trouble had been, when she'd gotten it out of him, she'd no longer been interested.

"Oh, all right," she finally said. "I might as well tell you the truth. You're bound to find out about it sooner or later."

Tom heaved a sigh of relief and sat down. The sooner she got whatever she had on her mind out of her system, the sooner he could get her to leave.

"I'm engaged to be married."

Tom's hopes took a leap upward. For the first time since he'd laid eyes on her, he smiled.

"Congratulations. Who's the lucky guy?"

"What difference does it make?" Obviously annoyed at his reaction, she went on. "All that matters to me is that my fiancé has said he'd like to have children."

"So, go ahead. Have as many as you like," he

answered. "But what does that have to do with your being here tonight?"

"Everything." A faint blush came across her face as she continued. "After what I went through in order to have Beth, I'm afraid I can't have more kids. It was hard enough at thirty-two, and I *am* five years older now." Her eyes narrowed as she studied him. "Unless, of course, *you* were the problem."

Tom fought to keep his temper. "Come off it, Jody. You know damn well the tests were inconclusive. The clinic's final report wound up as 'undetermined infertility.'" He took a deep breath, forcing himself to stay calm. If Jody was baiting him, she was out of luck. "The fact remains, there's Beth. What in the world does this have to do with her?"

"I've decided that if I bring Beth into the marriage, at least part of the year, my fiancé would be satisfied."

"No way!" Tom exclaimed. Now that she'd told him what she was after, he was more determined than ever to get rid of her. "If you think you're taking Beth anywhere, think again."

"Peter's wealthy," she protested. "He can give her a good home and everything she wants."

Tom exploded.

"Beth already has a good home. Right here with me! And she already has everything she wants!"

Her lips tightened, her gaze remained determined. He recognized the signs that Jody had dug in her heels. She was the same old Jody, not a damn bit different, just as he'd thought.

"You know," she added confidently into his silence, "if it comes to that, any court will recognize a mother's right to see her child. Especially when the child is being raised by a single man and when the mother has remarried and can provide her with a wholesome environment."

"What the hell is wrong with the environment around here?" he demanded.

Her gaze swept him with a suggestive look. "You certainly are a red-blooded man when you want to be. I remember that much."

He remembered that part of their marriage, too. It had been the only aspect of their relationship she'd been interested in. Until her interest had cooled and she'd looked for greener pastures. He could barely contain his anger. "What in the hell are you driving at?"

"Simply, who knows what influences a child could be subjected to in a home where her father might be entertaining a lady friend?"

"Come on, Jody, you're barking up the wrong tree. You know damn well I'm not the type to play around. You should have known I'd never agree to sharing Beth with you or anyone else."

"Nevertheless, I want part-time custody of our daughter after I'm married," she said, her false good humor gone. "I'm sure you'll come around once you've had time to think about it."

She wanted him to think about some other man raising his daughter? His mind recoiled at the thought.

"In your dreams, lady."

"Think about it, anyway," she answered brightly. "It will be better for all of us if you and I can come to an amicable settlement."

Tom shook his head. There wasn't any use in arguing with her, not when she wasn't prepared to listen.

He pitied the man Jody was going to marry. With that one-track mind of hers, the guy was in for a rough time. He remembered his own experience too well.

"I'm so tired, Tom," she said as she covered a yawn. "Why can't I spend the night?"

He regarded her steadily. Short of throwing her out bodily, it looked as if there was nothing he could do to get rid of her tonight.

"Since you're so determined to stay here tonight, go ahead and find yourself a bedroom," he finally said. "But just for tonight! And remember, if Beth agrees to it, a possible visit is all you're going to get."

After making sure Jody was settled in the back bedroom she'd chosen, Tom began pacing the floor. Too bad he hadn't changed the locks before this, but he intended to now. No way was he going to have Jody come in again uninvited. Hell would have to freeze over first.

She wanted to take Beth with her when she remarried, did she? he thought as he put Jody's coffee cup into the dishwasher. Hell, who knew how long Jody's next marriage would last, anyway? Beth wasn't a rubber ball to be tossed back and forth between her home and his.

Minutes later, the realization struck him that he'd done it again—he'd let his temper run away with his common sense. By allowing Jody to spend the night, he'd laid himself wide-open to any devious plans she might have. He wouldn't put it past her to claim they'd slept together to blackmail him into reopening Beth's custody case. The thought left him cold.

He had to move fast and stay a giant step ahead of her.

And now that he thought of it, before Jody had a chance to see that *both* Beth and Carly resembled her! Or before Laura had a chance to see Jody!

CARLY AND BETH shivered excitedly in the background while Laura searched her wardrobe for clothing Carly could wear to the doll's tea party. Her heart beat faster at the realization how close Tom Aldrich had come to accepting her impulsive invitation to join them. He would have been able to view her bedroom with all her intimate possessions...the very bed she slept in! The thought made her blush.

"How's this?" she questioned, holding up a short periwinkle-blue skirt and a filmy blue blouse to match. They were summer garments and the only usable items.

"I don't know, Mommy." Carly looked doubtful. "I don't think they'll fit Beth."

"They will after I get through with them," Laura replied. "See?" She knelt and held the skirt to Beth's waist. Thankfully, the skirt reached Beth's toes. "I'll take a tuck or two here and here. As for the blouse, I can fold under the sleeves, like so..." She demonstrated on a charmed Beth. "After we add a few bracelets, no one will be able to tell what's hidden under the jewelry."

"Shoes, Mommy! Beth needs shoes!"

Laura reached behind her and drew out a pair of

long-unused sequined, silver low-heel sandals. "There's an evening bag to match somewhere."

"And a hat," Carly squealed. "We both need hats and gloves!"

"Sorry," Laura smiled at her enthusiasm. "Gloves went out of style when I was a little girl. As for hats…we can make our own out of ribbons and feathers. How about that?"

"Cool." Carly giggled. Beth threw her arms around Laura and hugged her tightly. "Thank you, Mrs. Edwards!" she said shyly with tears in her eyes. "No one ever did anything so nice for me before."

Laura forced back her own tears as she felt a growing kinship with little motherless Beth Aldrich. Even though she was attracted to Beth's father, she sensed he somehow presented a threat to her and Carly. No matter, she thought as she returned Beth's hug, she could never turn her back on the little girl.

IN THE MORNING, Tom glanced uneasily at the closed bedroom door Jody had chosen for her own. He couldn't wait to get rid of her.

He heard a knock on the front door and glanced at his watch. It was too early for company. Maybe it was the replacement paper he'd called for when he'd found his own missing.

He shrugged into his flannel shirt and made for the door in bare feet. His heart skipped a beat when he heard giggles and whispers coming from the other side. Beth?

He said a brief prayer and opened the door. Laura, Beth and Carly stood smiling at him.

"I hope you don't mind my bringing Beth home."

Laura's eyes widened when she took in Tom's open shirt and unbuckled belt. The sight of his bare chest and his near state of undress took her by surprise. For a bewildered moment, she couldn't remember why she *had* agreed to bring Beth home instead of waiting for Tom to pick her up.

"Not at all," he answered, with a quick glance over his shoulder. "But first, I want—"

Laura found herself babbling to cover her embarrassment. "It's just that Beth was anxious to come home and show you the dress she picked to wear at the birthday party this afternoon."

She broke off when she heard a feminine voice call, "Tom? Who's there?" An auburn-haired woman wearing a sheer nightgown and little else appeared behind Tom. Laura felt herself flush.

The welcoming smile on Tom's face faded. He grimaced, shrugged an apology and whirled around to face the intruder.

"What the blazes do you think you're doing walking around like that in broad daylight?"

At his angry exclamation, a smile came over the woman's face. "Darling, how sweet of you to complain about my getting dressed. But I decided I really should put something on once I heard we had visitors."

Laura was struck by the sexual innuendo in the woman's voice. Far from complaining that his companion of the night had partially covered her nudity, Tom looked ready to explode.

Laura was stunned. And, from the look that came over the woman's face when she turned her gaze on Beth and Carly standing huddled together, so was she.

She hurriedly glanced down at the children. Frozen in place, Carly's eyes were wide as she stared at the woman whose curly auburn hair and green eyes were the same as Beth's. She had to be Jody, Tom's ex-wife.

To Laura's dismay, she saw Jody's eyes narrow with speculation and her glance dart between the two girls. Instinctively, Laura tried to put the children behind her, but not soon enough.

"Mommy?" Beth peeked around Laura and stared at her mother.

Laura's heart sank at the apologetic look Tom shot her. It was obvious from his expression he would have given anything for this not to have happened.

So would she.

She recalled the bits and pieces of information that Tom had dropped during their conversations. Brief details about his marriage to Beth's mother and the reasons for their breakup. Stories that had made her heart ache for the pain she saw in his eyes.

Lies.

Now that she saw the truth and a knowing look dawning on Jody's face, Laura realized she'd walked into a spider's web spun by a man who had deliberately wooed her friendship for an agenda of his own.

In order to get the information locked in the Eden clinic's records? Information that concerned Carly?

It was clear he hadn't needed the clinic's records to know that Carly was somehow related to Beth—and that this woman was surely their mother! A crushing weight filled Laura with fear.

Her knees shaking, the cold hands around her heart

robbing her of her breath, Laura's instinct was to grab her daughter and run.

Tom reached for her before she could turn away.

"Wait a minute! Laura, wait! I swear, it's not what you think!"

She hardened her heart at the anguish in his eyes and shook off his hand.

He was a good actor, she'd give him that, she thought bitterly. But he was also the man who, under the guise of wanting to share a friendship begun by their children, had lied to her about the state of his marriage. Why else would his ex-wife have spent the night with him?

"Don't go," Tom pleaded. "Please don't go. Not until I have a chance to explain. It's not what you think!"

Laura pulled away. "Don't bother. There's nothing to explain. I've seen enough." She urged Carly down the steps, hardening her heart to Tom's calls and Beth's cries for Carly to come back.

Tom cursed himself for letting Jody talk him into letting her spend the night. His first instinct was to run after Laura, to make her listen, to tell her the scenario she'd just witnessed had been deliberately planned by Jody to make their caller believe he and Jody had slept together.

He stopped short in his tracks when he realized Beth's reaction to seeing her mother had been anything but warm. That her cries hadn't been for her mother, but for Carly to come back.

Beth needed him.

Laura would have to wait.

When he bounded back up the steps, he found Beth

standing by the doorway frozen in place, staring at her mother.

"What did you say to Beth?" Tom demanded. He picked up Beth and cradled her against his shoulder.

"Just that I'm her mother," Jody told him, "but she doesn't seem to understand."

"Because she *doesn't* understand, dammit," he said between clenched teeth. "You left before she was old enough to have bonded with you. For her, you're no more than a figure in a framed snapshot." He cradled Beth in his arms and murmured, "It's okay, pumpkin. Don't be frightened. This is your mother."

Beth buried her face in his shoulder. "Is she really my mommy?"

"Yes, sweetheart, she is," Tom replied tenderly. "Don't you remember the picture you have of her in your room?"

Beth peeked out at Jody and nodded. "Is she going to come back and live with us?"

"No," he answered, sending a warning look over her head before Jody could answer for herself. He wasn't going to take a chance that Jody might frighten Beth. "Your mother is just here to visit."

"Now, wait a minute," Jody began. "I want—"

"What you want doesn't make a difference," Tom snapped. "How do you expect Beth to understand you're her mother when you come waltzing in here unannounced?"

"Well, I am," she answered defiantly, "and that's all that matters."

"No," Tom replied, thoroughly disgusted at the way things were going. "There's more to this and you know it. But I don't want to discuss it now—not in front of Beth. Why don't you go and get dressed while I try to explain your sudden appearance?''

''Okay, but Beth is my daughter, and don't you forget it.'' With a last triumphant glance at him, Jody swept regally out of the room.

Tom carried Beth into the living room and sank into the large upholstered chair where he read to her every night. The time they spent before he tucked her into bed became more precious with every passing day.

He put a finger under Beth's chin and gently lifted her teary face to his. Her innocent green eyes questioned his; her small mouth trembled. He swore silently. How could anyone do this to an innocent child?

She'd been so happy just yesterday, he thought sadly. What kind of father was he to have allowed Jody to upset her so? And just when Beth was so happy with her newfound friend.

He damned himself for allowing Jody to get the better of him. He should have carried her out bodily, if necessary, deposited her in a hotel and forbidden her to return before he'd had a chance to explain her presence to Beth.

He heard the sound of water running. Jody's scent drifted through the bathroom door. With her safely in the shower, he had some time to prepare Beth for the visit Jody wanted.

''Beth, sweetheart, look at me.''

Her woebegone expression as she focused on him almost took his breath away. He had to fight back the tears that threatened to come into his own eyes.

"Your mother got lonesome for you, pumpkin. She just didn't realize you might have forgotten her," he alibied, "or she never would have come back without calling and talking to you first."

"Why did she come back, Daddy?"

How could he tell her the truth when his thoughts were still in a turmoil after hearing Jody's threats to go to court to ask for part-time custody of their daughter? Plans that his gut told him spelled trouble for everyone, especially Beth?

Beth was still an innocent little girl who lived in the world of make-believe. No matter what it took, he wasn't going to allow that world to be taken away from her.

"I told you, pumpkin. Your mother discovered she missed her little girl," he answered.

"Then why did she go away and leave me before?"

Why, indeed? he wondered as he lovingly brushed the auburn curls away from Beth's forehead. How could anyone, let alone a mother, walk away from such a sweet child?

"I guess she thought she had some important things to take care of," he answered. He couldn't tell her Jody had decided reactivating her career was more important than her family. He hadn't understood the Jody of two years ago, he couldn't understand her now.

"More important things than you and me?"

He shook his head.

"People make mistakes, sweetheart. Sometimes they realize what they've done wrong and try to make things better."

Beth seemed to think about that for a moment. She finally sighed. "I guess it's like having to grow up, isn't it, Daddy?"

"Yes, like having to grow up," he agreed as he buried his lips in her curls. Beth was more perceptive than he'd realized. He tickled her under her chin until she started to giggle. "How about you? Are you going to stay my little girl or are you in a hurry to grow up?"

"I'll always be your little girl, Daddy," she assured him seriously. "Even after I'm grown-up."

He bent to kiss her pert little nose. "That's my girl."

"But what about Mommy? What did she mean when she told you to remember I'm her little girl, too?"

"Don't think about it, sweetheart. Everything is going to be okay," he replied. "We'll just take one day at a time and see where we go from here. Just remember I'm here for you, and don't you forget it."

He held Beth against his chest and rubbed her back until, exhausted with her emotions, she dozed off to sleep. "Here" was only a starting place. If he had anything to say about it, "here" was going to be the ending place for Jody's plans.

Beth finally stirred and awakened with a start. "Daddy?"

"I'm right here, sweetheart," he assured her. "You must have been tired to fall asleep that way." He studied her normally rosy complexion that was pale with exhaustion. "What time did you and Carly go to bed last night?"

"We went to bed at nine o'clock. But we didn't go to sleep until after midnight!" she crowed proudly.

"After midnight? That's *real* late!" Tom pretended surprise. "What were the two of you doing staying up so late?"

"Just talking. We have lots of things to talk about." She stopped to think. "Did you know that Carly has a mommy cat? And that she has babies? Lots of babies."

"No!" Tom answered with a straight face. He'd never considered having a pet around the house before, but he sensed he was about to have one now. Anything to make Beth happy.

"Carly says I can have one of the babies, if it's all right with you. Is it, Daddy?"

"I'll bet you already have one picked out."

"Yes." She smiled. "The two we decided to keep are little twins. Just like Carly and me."

"Twins?" Tom's mental antennae quivered. Had the girls realized how much they looked alike? The next logical step would be for them to wonder why. "When did you and Carly decide you were twins?"

"It's only make-believe, Daddy." She giggled. "We can't be twins because we each have different mommies and daddies. But last night we decided that since we look like each other, it might be fun to pretend we're twins. Isn't that funny?"

"Yeah, funny," he agreed.

Different mommies and daddies? Tom didn't know about that yet. But there was one thing he did know: He had to come up with a plan that would keep Jody from taking Beth away. And possibly Carly.

Chapter Six

Laura ignored Tom's calls to wait and bundled a bewildered Carly into the car.

Liar! She fumed as she drove away and left him standing in the street looking after her.

What kind of man was the real Tom Aldrich, she wondered through the tears that began to form.

He'd told her he was divorced and had dropped more than one hint that his marriage had been a disaster.

He'd traded on her sympathy and asked for help to learn how to be a better father.

He'd made her believe he was interested in her—not only as Carly's mother, but as a woman.

She'd found herself responding to his wicked, lopsided smile and the obvious interest in his eyes. Fool that she was, she'd even imagined herself held in his arms, pressed against his muscular body and drowning in his kiss!

All the time, it was obvious he'd been seeing his ex-wife, sleeping with her, making love to her!

And playing her—Laura Edwards, the woman who'd told herself this man could be the one man for her—for a fool! She hated him for his lies, and his hidden agenda—to take Carly from her.

But what had actually sent her into a panic was the realization that his ex-wife was an adult version of Carly!

Startled by the blast of a car horn in her ear and the irate face of the driver in the car next to hers, she realized she was driving erratically and putting everyone on the road in jeopardy.

"Mommy?"

The frightened sound in Carly's voice brought her to the present. Laura took a deep breath. "Yes, sweetheart?"

"Why did we have to leave Beth's house so fast? I know she wanted me to stay."

Laura's heart felt as though it were turning into stone.

"Because we were unexpected," she answered. "The polite thing to have done was to call and tell Mr. Aldrich we were coming." Even if it sounded like a lame excuse, at least it was partly true. She couldn't bring herself to voice the actual reason for her panic—the sight of Jody Aldrich. The one thing she was sure of was that she had to keep Jody from seeing Carly up close.

Out of the corner of her eye, Laura could see the lingering doubt on her daughter's face.

"Who was that lady in Beth's house?"

"I would guess she's Beth's mother," Laura replied, hoping Carly hadn't noticed her own resemblance to the woman.

A frown crossed Carly's forehead. "Are you sure?

I could tell Beth didn't like her. Besides, she told me she didn't have a mommy.''

Laura forced herself to smile, to hide her own fears.

"I'm sure you're wrong. What Beth probably meant was her mother and father are divorced, and that her mother doesn't live with them anymore.''

"I guess she lives with them now,'' Carly murmured. There was a pause. "Can Beth have two mommies?''

"Two mothers?'' Puzzled, Laura glanced at Carly. "Why would you ask such a question?''

Carly seemed to sink into the car seat. "I was just wondering, that's all.''

DISGUSTED WITH HIMSELF and worried about Laura's obvious reaction upon seeing Jody, Tom hugged his daughter close. Sooner or later, he intended to make certain Laura understood what had taken place hadn't been of his own choosing. He'd make her understand that there was no way in hell that he would reconcile with his ex-wife, let alone allow her to share custody of their daughter. He'd come too close to winning Laura's friendship to let Jody's appearance scare her off. And not only because of their children's resemblance, but because he'd found himself drawn to Laura for herself.

His immediate concern was to calm Beth's fears. He'd catch up with Laura later.

"Why don't you go freshen up,'' Tom told Beth when he'd had enough of worrying about what was going to happen next. "After you see your mother, we're going to visit Grandma.''

"Oh, Daddy, what about the party?'' she sighed.

Tom hated to do this, but he knew it was best for Beth. "Pumpkin, I'm sorry, but I don't think that's going to happen today."

As if she understood, Beth nodded. "What about Mommy? Is she coming with us?"

"No, I don't think so," Tom said, hardening his resolve to protect Beth from her mother. "Not this time."

Beth's childlike acceptance of her mother's reappearance in her life was touching. But how would she feel when she found out what Jody wanted?

Damn Jody anyway!

"Is Mommy going to be here when we get back?"

A closer look at Beth's face told Tom she wasn't as accepting of Jody's presence as he thought she was. "We'll have to wait and see, won't we? But I'm sure she won't be staying long. Now why don't you go and get ready?"

He hated to think about the meeting between Beth and her mother. With luck, maybe Jody would have the decency to see Beth was better off left in the security of the only home she'd known since she was born—his.

He paced the room, rubbing the back of his neck. This time, he intended to set Jody straight for once and for all. At the rate it was taking her to put herself together, he figured she was trying to look her best when she finally surfaced. Not that he gave a damn. The days when he couldn't wait to lay eyes on her, to hold her in his arms and make passionate love to her were long gone. He'd told her so last night. Too bad her ego wouldn't allow her to accept the truth—

that playing on her physical attraction wasn't going to get her Beth or anything else.

He heard the thud of the late newspaper delivery as it was thrown against the front door. Reluctant to leave Beth alone in the house with her mother, even for a few minutes, he glanced at the door to Beth's room. It was firmly closed, and unless he missed his guess, she wasn't going to come out any time soon. Not that he blamed her. When Jody had stormed out of the room in a fit of temper, he'd seen Beth wince.

He sighed and went to get the paper, then wandered into the kitchen to put on a pot of coffee. While the water dripped through the coffeemaker, he opened the newspaper and glanced at the front page.

His blood ran cold when he saw a follow-up story about the Eden Clinic. Although word of its alleged unethical practices had only just become public, it looked as if a disgruntled employee had blown the whistle some time ago. A secret investigation had been going on ever since.

From the gist of the article, he gathered he wasn't the only former patient of the clinic to suspect the unthinkable had happened. It appeared that someone had leaked the names of some of the clinic's patients and an investigative reporter hadn't wasted any time in interviewing them.

Would his name turn up? And if it did, what would it do to Beth and Carly?

He read on.

There were threats of a class action suit to force the clinic to provide DNA test results of former patients. And furthermore, to account for the way sperm, eggs and even embryos had been handled or used.

His blood ran cold as he read on. Authorities suspected that some children born as the result of the rumored thefts were being raised by couples other than their biological parents.

Tom could sympathize with anguished parents. After seeing Carly and Beth together and sensing Carly could somehow be his biological daughter, he was upset, too.

He considered his own case with a sense of relief. He, at least, was lucky to have found Carly the way he had. And luckier still, to find her being raised by a wonderful woman like Laura. The idea of placing that relationship in jeopardy and what it would do to the both of them twisted his gut.

The reporter was still looking for alleged victims. Tom prayed he'd never find him.

What finally floored him was that the article went on to say there were already couples set to go to court to get custody of children they believed were theirs. Some were even ready to sue for damages on the basis the rumors about the clinic's practices might turn out to be true. There was talk of being reimbursed for anguish and pain.

Anguish and pain!

Bells rang.

So that was what had brought Jody here!

She may have been honest about her forthcoming marriage, and her need to have Beth with her part of the time, but anguish and pain aside, she wasn't the type to pass the chance to cash in on an opportunity to get a settlement over Carly.

Troubled, he pictured Carly—a mirror image of Beth. If Jody had taken a good look at her, there'd be hell to pay. Her chances of getting custody of Carly were slim to none, but she'd sure as hell try.

The idea of their all winding up in court and its effect on the children left Tom cold.

He rued the day he'd met and fallen in love with Jody Towers, a long-legged, willowy redhead whose green eyes had tempted him from the moment he'd met her.

He rued the day he'd taken her to bed and let himself be drawn deeper and deeper into her sexual fantasies. After several months of living together, with Jody on her best behavior, he'd been fool enough to believe she wanted to spend the rest of her life with him. He'd ignored the warning signs of her single-minded determination to get whatever she wanted at the moment and, fool that he was, had asked her to marry him.

If Beth hadn't been the happy result, he would have regretted the day Jody had decided she wanted a child.

Naive jerk that he'd been, he believed it was every woman's right to have children if she wanted to. He hadn't realized that, once Jody had decided to be a mother, she'd be too stubborn to give up until she actually became pregnant. Or that, once she'd given birth to the baby she wanted, she'd become bored with motherhood. As far as he was concerned, Jody didn't have a maternal bone in her body.

He was tempted to tell her just how he felt and why. Except he didn't want to take the chance that she might take her anger out on Beth.

"Any coffee left in the pot?"

Newspaper clutched in his hand, he swung around

to face Jody. She was wearing a green-and-gold silk lounging caftan that matched her eyes. The neckline barely concealed her ample breasts. A matching headband held the auburn curls away from her temples, and a few tendrils had been artfully arranged to hang over her eyes. She looked as if she'd made a pilgrimage to Victoria's Secret.

This was definitely not her traveling outfit. She looked more as if she were ready to be taken to bed.

Where once he wouldn't have wasted any time taking her up on her blatant invitation, his instinctive reaction was to back away. He nodded without speaking.

"Well?" she asked, a knowing look on her face.

What she didn't realize was that a man *could* look and still not want to touch. He had to admire her tenacity, but she was wasting her charms on him.

"Aren't you going to pour me a cup of coffee?"

Tom took a fresh cup from the cupboard, filled it with freshly brewed coffee and silently handed it to her.

She reached for it with both hands, used one to take the cup and the other to lightly brush his hand. Tom smothered an oath.

"Cream?" she purred.

Barely managing to avoid her touch, he poured cream until she told him to stop.

"You wanted to talk, so talk," he said shortly. "And make it quick. I want you dressed and out of this house today."

She sank into a chair, crossed her legs and smiled. "Not without first seeing Beth. I intend to tell her I want her to live with me during the summer and on holidays. How I do it is up to you,'' she added suggestively. ''It all depends on whether or not you've decided to see things my way.''

''Daddy?''

Tom swore under his breath and bit off his terse reply. He'd been about to tell Jody to go to hell and that she'd never get her hands on Beth. The last thing Beth needed was to hear another argument; she'd seen and heard more than enough for one day. It would be better for all of them if Beth and her mother met amicably, and parted the same way.

''Hi, pumpkin,'' he said as he went to meet her. ''Your mother has been waiting for you. Come on,'' he coaxed. He took her cold hand in his and led her over to Jody. ''Let's say hello.''

He felt Beth's hesitance in the way she gripped his hand. He shot a warning glance in Jody's direction.

''Don't you remember me?'' Jody asked when Beth came to a reluctant halt in front of her.

Beth politely shook her head. ''No. But I have a picture of you in my room.''

''Good. Then you know I'm your mother, don't you?'' Jody smiled and reached for Beth. Beth drew back.

''Well, I am your mother,'' Jody continued with a defiant glance at Tom, ''and I came here to tell you I'll be seeing more of you from now on.''

More, hell, thought Tom. After not caring enough to visit her daughter in two years, even one more visit would be one too many. But Jody had made her intentions clear. If she had her way, she'd have Beth living with her and her new husband no matter what Beth wanted.

He was troubled by the thought of losing Beth, even for summers and holidays, and the negative effect it might have on her. He was even more troubled by the role Jody's new husband might play in Beth's life.

Would the guy appreciate the loving miracle that was Beth?

Would he want her to call him Daddy, too?

Never having had children of his own, would he have patience with her constant chatter?

Would he read to her before she went to sleep?

He glanced down at his daughter. Her eyes were as troubled as his own thoughts as they met his. He smiled his reassurance.

"Get on with this, Jody," Tom prompted with a warning glance over Beth's head. "But make it short."

For once Jody looked undecided. Tom relaxed. Maybe she *did* have a few mother's instincts after all.

"You can see Beth later and get reacquainted, if you both want to," he offered, stressing the word *both*. He wasn't going to let Jody pressure Beth into doing anything that might frighten her. "I'd already planned on taking Beth to see my mother at the convalescent home this afternoon, and I don't want to keep Mom waiting."

"Your mother? What's wrong with your mother?" Jody looked blank.

"She had a slight stroke two weeks ago."

"Oh. The last I heard she was taking care of Beth while you were away." Her measured glance shifted to their daughter. "Who's been taking care of her since then?"

''Yours truly,'' he answered with a short laugh. As if Jody were really interested in Beth's welfare. The only person Jody cared about was Jody.

''That must be interesting,'' she mused out loud. ''You never lifted a hand to help when she was a baby.''

The only reason Tom didn't blow up at the cutting remark was because it was true. But that was like the pot calling the kettle black—they were both guilty as sin.

He wasn't prepared to tell her about the promise he'd made to be a better father, to keep Beth safe and happy. And that it included protecting her from her mother, if necessary.

''Pumpkin,'' he said with a wary eye on Jody, ''maybe you ought to go into the den and call Carly. Tell her I said you can't make it today, but it's okay for you to adopt a kitten. And tell her we'll be over tomorrow to pick it up. Okay?''

Beth's eyes lit up. ''Cool, Daddy! I can hardly wait! Bye, Mommy,'' she said cheerfully and ran out of the room without looking back.

Tom pulled a chair from the table, straddled it and fixed Jody with a cold stare. ''I would have thought you'd have more sense than to try to start another argument with Beth around.''

''Oh, come on, Tom,'' she answered with a light laugh. ''It's so easy to rile you up, I just couldn't resist. But you weren't any more of a father than I was a mother. I guess the kid deserved more than the two of us for parents.''

Her smile was self-satisfied now that she'd made her point. He'd been a fool to fall into her trap. He stared into Jody's eyes and mentally counted to ten before he spoke.

"So, now that you've seen Beth, just what is it you really came here for?"

"I told you. I want to have her live with me, at least part-time. I simply can't gamble on being able to have another child. I *have* to have Beth." Her expression hardened, her eyes narrowed. "And furthermore, when the proper time comes, I don't want you to forget just who *is* her mother."

Tom's fragile nerves quivered. "And just what is that supposed to mean?"

She gestured to the newspaper that had fallen to the floor. "I've heard rumors the Eden Clinic is under investigation for mishandling embryos. And from what I gather, the allegations are true."

"So? What does that have to do with us?" He knew the answer all too well. He'd known it since her telephone call. His heart pounded as he waited for her answer.

Jody might not be the most astute woman in town, but she wasn't stupid, either. She'd obviously come to the same conclusions he had—that there was a possibility there were other biological children of theirs somewhere.

Icy fingers gripped the back of his neck. Carly!

Now that Jody had seen Carly and Beth together, it was just a matter of time their resemblance to each other and to herself would register and she'd try to cash in on it. Hell would break loose, and Laura's heart would be broken. She was bound to blame it all on him.

He took in the calculating look in Jody's eyes, the

satisfaction that came into them when she realized he understood her meaning.

He hadn't been mistaken about Jody, after all. She may have backed off on insisting on taking Beth for now, but she didn't have an ounce of motherhood in her. Not if she was willing to break another mother's heart for money.

The proof Jody needed to back up a claim that a test-tube embryo of theirs had been given to another couple had stared them all in the face when Carly had appeared at the door with her mother and Beth.

Sure, he'd wanted to solve the puzzle of the girls' similarity. But only to be in the position to help care for Carly if he turned out to be her biological father. As for Jody, she only wanted the children for window dressing.

He intended to stop her before she turned Laura's life into a living hell.

"Beth and I are going to leave now." He stood and stared down at Jody. "I don't want to find you here when we get back."

She shrugged her shoulders and picked up the newspaper.

"Why do you want money anyway?" Tom paused and asked as he followed her train of thought. "You said your fiancé is wealthy."

She shrugged. "Who knows how long the marriage will last?"

Tom turned away. All the more reason to keep her from getting her hands on Beth. He couldn't have her bouncing from home to home like a rubber ball.

As they drove away from the house, it was obvious

to him Beth was relieved to leave her mother behind. He felt damn good about it, too.

What Beth didn't know was that he was about to do something he'd sworn never to do again.

THE CONVALESCENT home where his mother was recuperating was a bright and cheerful place, but there was no disguising the fact that most of its patients were elderly. Please Be Quiet signs covered every entrance and every door. A medicinal odor filled the hall.

This for a woman who had declared her very existence depended on the sound of children's voices? Tom promised himself he'd take his mother home as soon as her doctors released her.

It might be a medical facility, but he was relieved to see someone obviously cared enough to get into a holiday mood. A Christmas tree decorated with red bows and silver bells occupied one corner of the entry. A bulletin board carried a notice that there would be a party for patients on Christmas Eve.

His mother was waiting for them. Before Tom could stop her, Beth threw herself across her grandmother's lap. "Guess what, Grandma! Daddy's going to let me have a kitten!"

"You don't say." His mother shared a happy smile with Tom. Her face glowed as she gently ran her fingers through Beth's curls. "Is it a little girl kitten or a little boy kitten?"

"She's a little girl like me," Beth bubbled. "Her name is Buttons, 'cause she has a small nose. And she has a twin, too, just like me. Only my twin's name is Carly."

Clearly puzzled, his mother glanced up at Tom. "A twin?"

"Yes." Lost in her own world, Beth answered happily, "Carly has the other one."

"I wasn't talking about the kitten, sweetheart," his mother said with a smile. "Who is this Carly?"

"I just told you, Grandma," Beth answered while she rummaged through her grandmother's knitting bag, "she's my twin."

"Twin? How could she be your twin, sweetheart?"

"'Cause we have the same color hair and eyes and we were almost born on the same day! We were both Christmas babies!"

"You don't say," her grandmother said again. "And that makes her your twin?"

"She's actually Beth's make-believe twin," Tom interjected with a warning glance at his mother. "It's a game they're playing."

"And not only that," Beth continued without a pause, "my mommy is staying at our house, Grandma." Beth paused for a moment. "Do you know her?"

Her grandmother's face whitened. Her smile disappeared and small worry lines appeared on her forehead. "Yes, I'm afraid I do."

"Don't you like her, Grandma?"

Tom groaned.

"You haven't reconciled with Jody, have you, Tom?"

He sat down beside his mother and took her soft hand in his. "No way, Mom. Don't even think about it. Jody just showed up out of the blue and refused to leave. When she told me she wanted to see Beth again, I had to let her stay long enough to visit. After all Jody *is* her mother.''

"Be careful, Tom," his mother warned with a sidelong glance at Beth. "If Jody gets so much as a foot in the door, she's bound to cause trouble." Her voice softened as she glanced down at Beth and gently stroked her bright curls. "The two of you don't need any more of that kind of heartache."

"I know," he reassured her. "I told her I didn't want to find her there when I got back home."

"Does that mean Mommy isn't going to live with us, Daddy?" Beth paused in her search through the knitting bag and looked up at Tom.

"No, she's not," Tom answered, realizing Beth shouldn't be listening to this conversation.

"Now, who *is* this Carly, son?"

"It's a long story, Mom, and I don't know if you're up to it. Why don't you wait and let me tell you about her when you come home?"

"It's not going to get any easier for you to tell me later or for me to be kept waiting to hear the story," his mother answered with more spirit than he'd seen in her in weeks. Growing up, when she'd used that tone on him, he'd known she meant business. From the look in her eyes, he knew she meant it now, too.

"Beth, why don't you go down to the nurse's station and see if she can scare up a soft drink for you while I talk to Grandma?"

"Sure, Daddy." She hopped off the bed, skipped to the door and, grinning, looked back. "Daddy wants to tell you a secret he doesn't want me to hear, Grandma. I'll be back when he's finished."

Tom and his mother exchanged rueful smiles.

''That child is sharp as a tack, son. I'm afraid nothing gets by her. Now, tell me the secret.''

Tom told her about Jody's plan to remarry and her threat to ask for divided custody of Beth. ''And as if that weren't enough, there's more,'' he added. He quickly told her about seeing Beth and Carly on stage together at the Beckwith Day School Christmas program, and his gut reaction to their astounding similarity.

He told her about meeting Laura at the school, and again at the Eden Clinic where he'd gone to try to solve the puzzle of the girls' possible relationship.

''That's certainly something to think about, isn't it?'' his mother said. She lay back against her pillows. ''But what would this Carly's mother think if her daughter actually turned out to be your and Jody's biological child?''

Tom repressed a shudder. The effect on Laura was too painful to think about. Thank God he had come up with plans to handle the possibility.

''Mom, would you mind if we left now? I promise we'll be back as soon as I've taken care of something important.''

''Carly?''

''Yes,'' he answered honestly. He didn't want to worry his mother, but, in some ways, she had a stake in this if she turned out to be Carly's grandmother. ''And her mother, too.''

His mother reached for his hand and searched his eyes. She finally nodded. ''This Laura must be a fine woman for you to care about her so much.''

''She is. As a matter of fact, she's more of a

woman than most I've known. And, to tell you the truth, I'm very attracted to her.''

In spite of impatience to get started, he paused to smile down at her. ''I know you'll take to each other when you meet. The two of you are a lot alike.''

''Am I going to meet her?''

''Yes, and soon. I promise.''

''Tom, promise me you'll stop to think carefully before you do anything rash. Don't let your anger at Jody rule your head.''

''I've already thought about it,'' he answered as he bent to kiss the worry lines away from her forehead. It wasn't his head he had to worry about; it was Laura's heart.

He walked out of the clinic strangely pleased with himself. The picture of Laura's smiling face flashed in front of his eyes.

Her lovely chestnut hair and hazel eyes had haunted his thoughts and more than a few of his dreams. The five little freckles that marched across her nose had enchanted him. Her slender, womanly figure had spoken to him of hidden fires. Fires he longed to share.

If he had his way, and provided she was willing, Laura Edwards was going to be more than a passing thought.

He intended to ask her to marry him.

Chapter Seven

By the time Tom returned home, Jody had decamped.
But not without leaving ample evidence of her brief
presence.

Her empty cup of coffee, ringed with the imprint
of her bright-red lipstick, remained on the kitchen table where she'd left it.

Damp towels were strewn over the bathroom and
her scent permeated the room. Her bed looked as if a
cyclone had blown through the room. Typical, he
thought sourly. She'd said she'd changed, but her
housekeeping sure hadn't improved.

He gathered up the used linens and loaded them
into the washer. He didn't want anything around to
remind him of Jody, hadn't wanted any part of her
from the day she'd announced she wanted a divorce.

By then, he'd already learned to live with her indifference, but the pain of ultimate rejection had still
hurt. Nothing he'd said or done had changed her
mind. She'd been just as determined to start a new
life without him as she had been determined to marry
him.

He hadn't cared so much for himself as he had for

their small daughter. Beth had been the answer to a prayer, a miracle, and everything any parent could have asked for. But once the excitement of her birth had worn off, Jody had looked for a new challenge. He again felt sorry for the poor sucker she was going to marry.

"Daddy?"

The unhappy note in Beth's voice concerned him. "What's up, pumpkin?"

"Mommy left me a note on my dresser." Beth looked puzzled. "What am I supposed to do with it?"

"Depends on what it says." Tom reached for the slip of paper and studied it for a moment. It was a telephone number written on a local hotel's stationery—ample evidence Jody had had a room nearby all the time she was trying to con him into allowing her to stay.

Not that spending the night in his house had done her much good.

"It's only a telephone number, sweetheart. There's nothing to worry you."

"Does it mean I have to call her?"

"Only if you want to," Tom replied. He knew the answer but he was careful to let Beth make her own decision. "Want to talk about it?"

When Beth nodded, he led her into the kitchen and sat down to listen. "Okay, pumpkin, out with it. What's wrong?"

"I don't think I want to call Mommy," she answered with a catch in her voice.

The raw appeal in her luminous eyes caught at his heart. He wanted to cradle her in his arms, to tell her she didn't have to do anything she didn't want to do.

But he knew it'd be wiser to let her talk it out. "Why is that, baby?"

He hadn't called her baby in a long time—not since she'd solemnly told him she was too old for the endearment. But she seemed so young, so vulnerable at the moment, he couldn't help himself.

"I'm afraid Mommy will take me away," she confided, her eyes shimmering with tears.

He wiped away a tear that spilled over onto her pale cheek. "No one's going to take you anywhere," he told her. "You're going to stay right here with me and Grandma. If you want to see your mother again, we'll just invite her over here. Would you like that better?"

He waited while Beth thought about his offer. The indecision on her face was enough to break his heart.

Damn Jody anyway! In spite of his attempts to keep Beth from hearing Jody's blatant threats, she must have overheard enough of their conversation to frighten her.

So much for his attempt to be fair. All he'd accomplished was to make Beth unhappy.

He should have made Jody leave the moment he'd come home and found her making herself at home.

The note reminded him that not only was he in danger of having to fight for his daughter, but that Laura might have to fight for hers, too. In Laura's case, she had more to lose than Carly, she'd lose her last link to the husband she'd loved and lost.

His first instinct was to crush the piece of paper and throw it where it belonged—in the trash. On second thought, he decided to keep it, just in case. For everyone's sake, he intended to keep an eye out for

Jody. He wasn't going to let her upset them all on a whim without a fight.

Beth sighed and looked at him wistfully. "I wish I could have a mommy like Carly's."

"Why is that, pumpkin?" He reached in his pocket for his handkerchief and wiped away another tear.

She smiled through her tears before she answered him. "Because she's nice and she makes me feel good."

Laura made him feel good, too, Tom thought as he returned his daughter's smile.

Now that he was actively working at it, and in spite of setbacks like today, he'd found he actually liked being an involved father. He'd discovered more about the pleasures of being Beth's dad in the past two weeks than he had since she'd been born.

There was the added dividend of rediscovering, through the eyes of a child, the everyday things in life he'd taken for granted. Each day, as seen through Beth's eyes, was a new and exciting adventure. He hugged her close and prayed that her tears would soon turn into smiles.

"How about pitching in and helping me make dinner?" he said, anxious to get Beth's mind on a happier subject.

Beth giggled. "The only thing Grandma lets me make are peanut butter sandwiches. Do you like peanut butter sandwiches, Daddy?"

"Love 'em," he declared. He hadn't willingly eaten one since he'd stopped being a kid, but he couldn't dampen Beth's pleasure. Or take away her growing look of confidence.

"But be sure and add some jelly," he cautioned,

careful not to mention the combination was the only way he'd ever been able to tolerate peanut butter sandwiches, and only if he were starved.

"Sure, Daddy," Beth answered. "But you'll have to open the jar. You're stronger than me."

As he followed her into the kitchen, he had to admire the way she unconsciously complimented him, fed his male ego.

After a dinner of sandwiches and a glass of cold milk, Tom decided to take care of a few important details.

"You can watch television while I clean up," he offered. "I'll be in in a few minutes."

"Grandma lets me help her clean up," Beth volunteered. "Don't you want me to help you?"

"Well, I figured that since you made dinner, I ought to do the dishes. Besides, your favorite programs are on tonight. Fair is fair, right?"

With a dimpled grin, Beth made for the den.

Tom headed for the telephone.

"Len? Sorry to bother you at home, but I figured it was safer than calling you at the office tomorrow."

"That's okay, I could use a break," Len's harried voice replied. "I was in the midst of trying to referee a game of Scrabble."

In the background, Tom heard sounds of heated arguments and calls for a dictionary.

"Things have heated up around here," Tom told him. "I wondered if you had a chance to talk to Manny yet."

"No, not yet. Hey, guys, I said keep it down! No not you, Tom, I was talking to the boys." He sighed. "Give me a break, it's only been a couple of days."

"Five," Tom corrected him. "I can't wait much longer. Not after trouble showed up last night."

"What kind of trouble?"

"Jody," he said succinctly. Len had been his partner for the past ten years and had seen and heard more than enough about Tom's marriage to understand the problem without further clarification.

"Jeez! What did she want?"

"Feels like everything," Tom told him. "Actually, it not only has to do with Beth, it's about Carly, too."

"Your other kid? That's a hell of a note! I figured you'd seen the last of Jody two years ago."

"So did I," Tom agreed. "But she says she's getting married again and wants partial custody of Beth to keep her new husband happy. Now that she's caught a glimpse of Carly, she'll probably want her, too."

"That's tough," Len agreed.

"So," Tom continued, "do you think you can persuade Manny to get me into the clinic's files in the next few days?"

"Truthfully, no. Not since the media began spreading the story big-time. Now that the word is out Manny's been quietly working on the case, they're hounding him for information. He's as jittery as a cat."

"Got any other ideas?"

"If you give me the names you're interested in," Len said with a whisper, "maybe I can persuade him to get copies of their DNA records and pass it on."

"That might work," Tom gave him Laura's and Carl's names. "Can you try to get on it right away?"

"Maybe. I'll have to wait for things to cool off before I approach him."

Tom's spirits rose a notch. "Maybe" just might be good enough if the information reached him in time for what he had in mind. "Thanks. Call me if you come up with any news."

He hung up the telephone. It was no longer solely a matter of finding out if he was Carly Edwards's biological father. Now there was the added problem of keeping Jody's hands off *both* the girls.

It looked as if he were on his own, at least for a while. No matter what the clinic's records might eventually reveal, he couldn't wait. He had to move on before Jody dropped the other shoe.

Maybe the only thing left to do was to corner Laura in the morning and to level with her. To tell her he knew about and shared her unspoken fears. And that he cared enough for her to want to protect her from any further pain.

THIS TIME, when he tried to get into the clinic, he wasn't so lucky. The receptionist was gone. In her place, there were two armed policemen—one at the front door and the other patrolling the entry.

"Sorry, sir. You can't come inside," the guard said politely. "What can I do for you?"

Tom took out his INS badge and flashed it at the guard. Maybe one law enforcement agency would bend long enough to show courtesy to another. "I need to look through some files for a case I'm working on."

The guard wasn't moved by the badge. "Got a court order?"

"No, I didn't have time to stop long enough to get one," Tom answered. He tried his official noncommittal smile.

"Sorry, no one is working today," the guard answered. "You might check back in a few days."

Tom didn't need to ask why no one was working today. From the looks of things, he knew he wouldn't have gotten an answer, anyway. With the parking lot almost empty, and a police car parked near the entrance, he should have known something was up. In all probability, a complete search of the clinic and an audit of its records were taking place.

Maybe, with luck, Laura would be at home.

"Thank you, I will," he answered. As he turned away, Tom could feel the guard's eyes piercing his back.

The enigmatic look on the guard's face had belied the look of steel in the man's slate-gray eyes. Without a court order, "no one" had meant him, too. Or was there something about him that had made the guy suspicious?

Maybe he shouldn't have shown his badge and told the man what he wanted.

To make him feel even more uncomfortable, it started to rain.

Damn! He had to restrain himself from taking giant steps to his car and getting out of sight before the policeman called him back.

He debated using his cell phone, calling Laura at home and asking if he could drop by. After her encounter with Jody, he wasn't all that sure Laura would welcome him. Still, he had to see her as soon as possible, tell her what he suspected and make her realize that they were both in jeopardy. That they *both* might lose their children to Jody, if only on a part-time basis.

It had started to rain in earnest by the time he pulled up to Laura's house. He tried to shelter himself from the wind-driven rain and rang the doorbell in quick staccato motions. When no one answered, he knocked impatiently on the door.

Laura pulled aside the curtains to see who was making all the racket. It was Tom Aldrich—definitely not a man she wanted to see. Not now, and after yesterday, maybe never again.

Torn by indecision, she bit her lip and tried to decide whether or not to open the door.

Even wet and bedraggled, he made her heart race. He was that rare man who wasn't ashamed to show emotion, to feel, to care. He was a man who had touched her soul.

She'd realized almost right away there was a growing attraction between them. It hadn't taken long for her to feel an emotional and physical response to his frankly interested gaze. And, even though she'd been furious with him a short time ago, she felt that response even now.

He might be all the things a woman could ask for in a man if she were asking, but Laura was afraid to let herself ask. She didn't need to add more trouble in her already troubled thoughts.

Still, he looked so wet and miserable, she didn't have the heart to leave him standing in the rain. She opened the door just wide enough to look him over. "What do you want?"

"I have to talk to you."

"As long as you're here, you might as well come inside," she said, questioning her common sense. He didn't look as if he were in any condition to go anywhere. "You can dry out in the kitchen."

"Thanks." He stopped and looked down at his feet. "I guess I should take off my shoes before I ruin the rug."

She nodded and closed the door behind him. "How did you know I was home?"

"I checked at the clinic," he answered, bending over to untie his shoes. He wiped the water from his face, only to have new raindrops fall from his hair. "When I was told it was closed, I figured I'd find you here."

"What have you come for?" she asked reluctantly. She didn't think she'd gotten an honest answer from him yet, but there was an urgent look in his eyes that told her he just might be truthful with her now. She led him into the kitchen.

The smell of spices and brown sugar filled the room. She noticed the hungry look that passed over Tom's face as he eyed a tray of baked cookies cooling on the table.

"I was in the midst of baking cookies for Carly to take to school tomorrow. Go ahead and talk." She picked up a cookie cutter shaped like a Christmas tree and set to work. "In the meantime, maybe you ought to take off that jacket," she said after a glance at the uncomfortable way he looked. "And that shirt. You look soaked."

Tom shrugged off his jacket with a grateful smile. He glanced down at his wet shirt, shot her an apologetic grin and peeled it off. His T-shirt was damp.

She gazed at his broad shoulders and the muscles that rippled sensuously as he dried off his hair with a kitchen towel.

Thank goodness he didn't take the T-shirt off, Laura thought as she rolled the cookie dough with more force than was necessary. There was already enough of him showing to tempt a saint.

At this rate, she wasn't going to be able to concentrate on her baking.

Once seated at the table, she noticed his hungry glance at the tray of freshly baked cookies.

"Help yourself. I'll have these in the oven in a minute."

He reached for a cookie. The smile that had first attracted her was back. So was the warm feeling in her middle.

"Why don't you take off your socks? They look pretty damp. You can dry them out by the oven."

"Thanks, I'd appreciate that," he answered with a smile. He sat down, peeled off his wet socks and hung them over the back of a chair.

Why had she suggested he do that? Laura chided herself as she watched him pad back to the table in his bare feet. She was having enough trouble keeping her mind off the parts of him that were already exposed.

She put the cookie tray in the oven to bake, filled two cups with coffee and joined him at the table.

"What was it you wanted to speak to me about?"

The grim look that replaced his smile sent shock waves through her. With an inward shudder, she sensed that whatever he was about to tell her wasn't going to be something she wanted to hear.

"Is something wrong?" When he didn't answer, she felt herself grow pale. She started to rise. "Is it Carly? Is she hurt?"

"God, no!" He grabbed her hand. "I did want to talk to you about Carly, but I'm sure she's all right. She *is* in school, isn't she?"

"How could you frighten me like that?" she demanded, sinking back into her chair. "You took ten years off my life!"

"I'm sorry. I never meant to." His grim look remained.

Laura's senses jumped to full alert. From the concern in his eyes, she sensed nothing good could come of what he was about to tell her. The ominous feeling inside her grew until it threatened to envelop her.

How could she have become attracted to this man, she wondered. Strangers from two different worlds, they might never have met and become attracted to each other under normal circumstances. She spent her days in a back office buried in paperwork. She sensed he lived in a more dangerous world.

Mesmerized by the intensity of his gaze, she waited.

"To start with," he began quietly, "I hope you can believe my reason for coming here isn't meant to hurt you or Carly in any way."

She listened intently while he told her about seeing Beth and Carly together on stage at the school's *Nutcracker* presentation and his reaction to the girls' similarity. He told her he had actually laughed and decided it was a chance resemblance.

He wasn't laughing anymore.

"What are you driving at?" she asked. A wave of apprehension swept over her.

"To be frank, I've since decided there must be some biological connection between Beth and Carly."

"Don't be ridiculous, how could there be?" she answered, even as bits and pieces of the possible answer came together in her mind.

"You've thought so all along, haven't you? Is that why you kept showing up at the clinic?"

"To be honest with you, at first, yes," he answered. "But when I saw the newspaper headlines about the practices at Eden, I was almost positive. Weren't you?"

She was. The hope she'd been wrong faded at his question. She shook her head. She couldn't bring herself to tell him her own fears had crystallized after reading the same headlines. It would only convince him that his suspicions were true.

She'd wanted to take Carly and run when she'd first realized she might be involved in the clinic's switch of embryos and its significance. She wanted to run now.

Laura felt the tears she'd been struggling to hold back start to trickle from the corners of her eyes. She wiped them away with the back of her hand.

"Laura," he continued, "I never intended to hide my reasons for showing up at the clinic the first time. Surely by then you must have suspected why I was there?"

Willing away her tears, she gazed at him and wondered how much more of this heartache she would have to bear.

Her silence condemned her.

"Please believe I'm not the devil trying to take your daughter from you. It's just that I had to find out if I could possibly be Carly's father."

"How dare you?" She pulled her hand free from his. "Carly's father is my husband, Carl!"

"I wouldn't have wanted to take that away from her," he protested. "I only wanted to be there for her in case she needed me. And to be there for you, too."

His eyes spoke of things she couldn't afford to hear. Even through the fear that enveloped her, an answering emotion shot through her at the tender look in his eyes.

He was a reminder of sad and happy memories, she thought sadly as she gazed at him. Of years of believing she was barren, and the joy of finally finding she was pregnant. Of the sorrow of losing her late husband weeks before the baby's birth, and the comfort of knowing he'd left a part of him behind in her beloved Carly. If what Tom was suggesting was true, she'd lose the last tie she had to Carl.

Unable to bear her thoughts, she looked away to the familiar sight of the ceramic figures Carly had made in a craft class for Laura's birthday. To her coffee cup with Carly's picture on it she had made in the mall last year at Christmas. And to all the things that spoke of her life here with her beloved and precious daughter.

Tom was a threat to all she held dear. If he was suggesting they might have a future together, it was hopeless. What kind of a future would there be with a man she couldn't trust?

"I can't discuss this with you any longer," she

answered. "You're mistaken. All of that is coincidence. My late husband *is* Carly's father. Now that you've told me what you came for, please dress and go."

"I can't, not yet," he pleaded. "I'm afraid there's more to this than I've told you."

"Haven't you said enough?" she asked bitterly. "What more could you want?"

"I wish I didn't have to tell you this, but I have to," he answered. "There's no way to break it to you gently. Your late husband may have been Carly's father, but if he was, then my ex-wife has to be her biological mother."

Laura exploded. "You're out of your mind!"

"No. I wish I was wrong, but you saw Jody. You have to know it's true."

"That's impossible!" Laura cried. "Carly *is* my daughter! I gave birth to her!"

"You may have given birth to her, but if Carly was conceived in vitro, anything could have happened," he said quietly. "She *was* a test-tube baby, wasn't she?"

Laura fought her tears. "Yes, she was." There was no use lying. He was bound to find out the truth, anyway. The in vitro process she and Carl had gone through before Carly's birth was something she couldn't hide. Not when the clinic's practices had become public knowledge, and not from a determined man like Tom Aldrich.

The only truth she knew was that she'd given birth to her daughter. Had she only been a surrogate mother? she wondered, holding in her fears. Did the child she'd so lovingly carried for nine months belong to someone else?

"Laura, you have to believe I have no intention of allowing anyone to take Carly away from you. No matter who her biological mother and father were. That's why I'm here."

"You and your wife," she said bitterly.

"My ex-wife," he corrected. "I haven't had anything to do with her for years. In fact, until yesterday, I hadn't seen her since our divorce."

"That's not what it looked like when I brought Beth home!"

She'd been shocked at the sight of Jody dressed in a sheer, seductive nightgown and Tom looking half dressed. Not because she had been jealous, but because, for the first time in six years, she was attracted to a man and had been foolishly pleased that Tom was obviously attracted to her. It had been more than jealousy. She'd felt betrayed.

"That was Jody playing for an audience," he said. "She appeared out of nowhere, and spent the night in my guest room. And that's another thing we have to talk about."

The smell of burning cookie dough filled the room.

"Oh, good Lord, I've let the cookies burn!" Laura grabbed two pot holders, reached into the oven and pulled out the tray of burning cookies. "Now look at what I've done!"

She dropped the smoldering tray into the sink, covered her eyes and tried to muffle the sobs that overwhelmed her.

Tom started for her. All the tender emotions he felt for Laura surfaced. He put aside his own concerns and took her into his arms. The protective feeling that came over him whenever he managed to hurt Laura came over him now.

"Don't cry, Laura," he murmured. "They're only cookies. You can make some new ones. I'll even help."

"I'm not crying over the cookies," she sobbed into his almost bare chest.

"I know," he said tenderly. "It's about Carly, isn't it?"

"Yes. I don't care what you want to believe, I *am* her mother," she added fiercely.

"Of course you are," he said into soft hair scented with the odor of burnt chocolate cookies. "In all the ways that count. Why don't you turn off the oven and come back and sit down. We have some serious planning to do."

While she dried her eyes, Tom told her about Jody's threats to go to court to get partial custody of Beth—or worse. And the sexual innuendos she'd pulled on him when she spoke about the danger of a female child living with a single father.

"If she saw how much you cared for Beth as I did, how could she think of such a thing?"

"I wouldn't put anything past Jody," he answered, encouraged by her remark. Maybe his case wasn't hopeless. He took a deep breath. "I'm also afraid she's going to use the striking resemblance between the girls and herself in court."

Laura went still with shock. Her stomach churned, her blood ran cold. She felt as if she were standing on a precipice, and that without Tom's arms around her she would pitch forward into darkness.

"If the rumors turn out to be true, I'm afraid it's possible that the clinic's doctors switched sperm and eggs at will between patients," he continued. "I believe they took one of Jody's fertilized eggs and implanted it in you."

"Oh, my God!" Shock dried her tears. "You don't actually think Jody will try to take Carly away from me, do you?"

"I'm afraid I do," he said, "although I don't think she has a chance. She told me she needs to bring children to her upcoming marriage and that she's afraid she can't have any more. She also hinted she'll use her biological ties to Beth and Carly to sue the clinic's doctors for the emotional distress they caused her."

"What am I going to do? I can't let Carly be subjected to all of that." She stood and looked around her distractedly. "I've got to find somewhere to hide until this is over. For Carly's sake more than my own. It would break her heart if she thought I wasn't her mother."

"Well," he replied, "I had an idea." He stood, went to her side and hesitantly brushed her damp cheek with a gentle forefinger. "I've thought of one way we can put a crimp in Jody's intentions. That is, if you're willing to put your trust in me."

Laura gazed at him through unshed tears. Trust him? The circumstances made him the last man she should trust. But she had nowhere else to turn, no one else to turn to except her sister, Dina. And she couldn't think of a way Dina could help her.

The intent look in Tom's eyes and the tender way he was stroking her cheek determined her. She couldn't turn him down without at least listening to him, to gamble they were both on the same side.

"What do you suggest I do?"

"You could marry me."

Chapter Eight

Laura gasped. "What did you say?"

"I said, you could marry me," Tom repeated.

"Why, for heaven's sake?"

"Because I'm convinced it would solve both our problems."

"I can't believe you're serious!" She looked at him as if he were the devil. "How can you joke at a time like this?"

"I've never been more serious about anything in my life," he answered. He tried to appear calm; inside he felt as tense as a drum. He wasn't sure he could handle it if she turned him down.

He could understand her surprise. When the thought had occurred to him that if they were married, he and Laura would present a formidable defense against anything Jody might come up with, he'd been surprised, too. But the longer he'd considered the idea, the better it had sounded.

He hadn't been able to come up with another scenario and besides, time was running out. If Laura didn't go along with him, they were both going to be in deep trouble.

"Let's back up a minute," he said when she didn't look convinced. "Jody told me she intends to remarry soon so we can't put our own marriage off. We have to beat her to the punch before she tries something stupid like trying to get custody of Beth—and Carly, too."

The frown on Laura's forehead deepened.

"I don't understand how our getting married could stop her."

"Look at it this way," Tom argued reasonably. "If we married, as the girls' parents, we would be in a better position to protect them from Jody."

Laura looked bewildered. He could understand that, too.

"It's all in the matter of how the clinic switched donor embryos and 'sold' them to other patients," he continued. "I know it sounds involved, and maybe even ridiculous, but the bottom line is that by marrying, we'll ensure the girls will be raised together."

Satisfied with his logic, he sat back and studied Laura's reaction. Her face was flushed, whether from baking cookies or from his unorthodox proposal, he didn't know. But from her frown, it was obvious he still hadn't convinced her. Reasonable or not, the thought of marriage to him seemed to have left her cold.

Maybe he should have been more tender, less logical, maybe even romantic, but he had been afraid he'd scare her off. She was wary enough of him as it was.

"Besides," he added quickly while he still had her attention, "I figure the courts would be more sympathetic to our position as a family unit than to Jody's. At least until she got married.''

''You're sure about that?''

''As for Carly, yes. I don't remember ever hearing about a situation like this happening before, but I don't think Jody would have a legal leg to stand on if she tried to take Carly away from us. Not when I'm probably her father to begin with.'' He waved a fresh cookie at her. ''I'm sure there's no precedence for a case like ours, at least not yet. It's going to take years before these cases are settled. Who knows what might happen by then?''

Laura still looked thoughtful. He had to try harder.

''Actually, the marriage would be more for Carly's sake than Beth's. In Beth's case, Jody turned down shared custody before. I don't think any judge would pay much attention to her change of heart now.''

''I wouldn't have believed this if I hadn't heard it with my own ears,'' Laura muttered distractedly.

Tom breathed a sigh of relief. It looked as if her initial distrust and fear of him had been shocked out of her.

Gazing at the loveliness that was Laura, he wished his proposal of marriage could have come later, after they'd had a chance to get to know each other better. That it could have been for any other reason than this. That he could tell her he realized how traumatic Jody's appearance and her threats were for her. And for him, too. He watched the changing expressions on Laura's face go from tears to anger.

Good, Tom thought, anger was easier for him to handle than the tears that had been Jody's defensive weapon. Maybe now they could move on.

While Laura seemed to consider his marriage proposal, her eyes bored right through him. Could she possibly tell he already had someone probing the clinic's records without waiting for Jody's next move? Would she think his marriage proposal was a ruse of his to take Carly away from her? He shifted uneasily.

"Let me get this straight," she finally said. "You're saying the reason we should get married right away is to keep the girls out of Jody's clutches?"

"Yes, among other things," he said impulsively before he caught himself. Where had *that* come from, he wondered, taking a good look at Laura. He'd been so deep in trying to logically explain his reasons for their marriage, he hadn't stopped to realize just how much he'd actually begun to care for her. How much he wanted to caress her satin skin, to taste her rosy lips and to feel her body pulse with desire as he held her to him. He felt her attraction so strongly, it was all he could do to keep himself from reaching for her and showing her how much he actually did care for her.

"*What* other things?" Laura's eyes narrowed again. Clearly, her suspicions were back.

Tom pulled his thoughts together and tried to think of an answer that would satisfy her.

He couldn't claim to be falling in love with her; she'd never believe him. Not after a beginning like theirs.

"To start with, let me say I actually admire and respect you. And although it's true that after my experience with Jody, I hadn't planned on ever marrying again, it seems to be the wisest thing to do now."

He couldn't tell her it had taken him years to get over the blow to his ego of his ex-wife announcing she'd lost interest in him and their marriage. His ego had taken enough blows to last a lifetime. Or that he and Jody had remained together for Beth's sake while they drifted further and further apart until she'd walked out. In retrospect, his attempts to keep the marriage together for their daughter's sake had been a big mistake. Jody's indifference must have hurt Beth more than he realized, or she would have been happier to see her mother again.

But that was then, and this was now. Laura was no Jody. Laura's character and honesty, caring ways and her love for her daughter were genuine.

He eyed Laura warily. Things had changed, for the better, he hoped. "For another thing, we like each other—at least we did until Saturday. That's a good starting point. Maybe we can learn to like each other again. Right?"

"Maybe." She started to gather up the mixing bowl, measuring cups and spoons before she paused and reminded him, "Liking someone isn't a good enough reason to get married. Most people like the things that aren't good for them."

Clearly, "maybe" wasn't going to be good enough.

He glanced around the homey kitchen and drew in the scent of freshly baked cookies. Freshly starched white curtains framed the windows, small pots of tropical plants and lopsided ceramic animals, clearly made by a child, filled the garden window. A pot of soup simmered on the stove.

It may have been cold and rainy outside the house, but inside, the kitchen reflected the loving warmth he'd come to associate with Laura. A warmth he wanted to share more than he'd realized when he'd first thought of the marriage scenario. He took a deep breath and plunged on.

"For another thing, you're a good mother."

"And that's supposed to be a basis for marriage between us?" she asked incredulously.

He wanted to say yes. After Jody, a good mother was high on his priority list. Clearly, Laura needed more than that. "That's only a part of it," he answered.

"Well," she said, dropping the baking utensils into soapy dishwater, "let me tell you that trying to keep me from losing Carly is one thing, but marriage to you is another!"

From the scornful expression on her face, he knew he had to come up with a better reason and damn quick.

Maybe now wasn't the time to tell her how cute she looked with a smudge of chocolate cookie dough across her forehead and her face flushed from baking—or was it anger? That the scent of chocolate cookies that clung to her was more intriguing than any perfume she could have worn. To tell her how he'd been drawn to her smile the first time he'd noticed her. Or that, heaven help him, he'd gone well beyond being merely attracted to her. She even made his body stir with desire whenever he looked at her.

He had the sinking feeling that if he had intended

to voice those thoughts, he should have done it before this. From the way things were rapidly going downhill, she'd never believe him now. She was bound to think he was making them up to get her to agree to marrying him. On the other hand, she might even think he was coming on to her. In her present mood, that clearly wasn't a good idea.

"Okay," he said, shaking cookie crumbs from his fingers. "Let's get down to business. To begin with, I'm sure there has been more than one marriage made for lesser reasons than ours."

Her frown suggested he could be wrong.

"As far as I'm concerned," he added as he rose and paced the kitchen, "Beth and Carly deserve a better life than any Jody can give them. And a mother and father who love them." He stopped to confront her. "That means you and me. I'm willing to fight for the girls—how about you?"

He thought he'd finally gotten through to her, until he saw a wary look come into her eyes.

"How much of a marriage would this marriage be?" she finally asked. A furious blush came over her face.

Tom blinked. For the first time since he'd come up with the marriage idea, he'd begun to think of Laura as the woman who would actually be his wife. The woman to whom he would come home to at night, the woman who could be the mother of his future children.

The words of the marriage ceremony, *to have and to hold from this day forward,* flashed into his mind.

What in the hell was *to have and to hold* supposed to mean under the present circumstances?

Laura silently studied the expressions that crossed Tom's face. Not that she expected much from him. He was, after all, a man who had just called marriage a business. If that's all he thought marriage was, no wonder Jody had looked elsewhere.

How would he feel after they were married—would he actually treat her only as a partner in a business proposition or not a partner at all?

What kind of marriage would it be, she wondered as she waited while he fought to come up with an answer. A cold-blooded union of two people who'd gotten married for the sake of their respective children? Two people trapped in a marriage of convenience?

No way! As far as she was concerned, marriage was for life and for love.

After Carl had died in the automobile accident, she thought she'd learned to live without a husband's love. Things had changed when she'd met Tom. After she'd seen the loving way Tom took care of his daughter and worried about his mother, she'd begun to see him in a different light—as a woman looks at a man. Her mind and her body had awakened to what she missed—someone to hold her, to love her, to share her fears and her dreams. To father her children.

She'd told herself she was too old to believe in fairy tales or that a Prince Charming would come out of the blue to ease the empty place in her heart. Had she been wrong? Was Tom that prince?

Did she have another choice than to marry him if she wanted to protect Carly?

Tom's voice broke into her thoughts. ''Look, Laura, why don't we get married and take this one step at a time? Why not let the future answer any questions about the path our marriage might take?''

Laura closed her mind to her yearning heart. One step at a time wasn't good enough. Not when she seemed to be on the verge of falling in love with a man who didn't know the meaning of the word. She had to find a different way to protect Carly.

''I'm sorry,'' she said. ''If I agree to marry you, I'd have to know in advance how much of myself I'm expected to give. And how much of yourself you're willing to give me in return. I can't afford to wait until it's too late to turn back.''

She yearned to have him tell her she was mistaken. To tell her he could learn to love her, just as she would try to love him in return.

For a moment, Tom seemed to be lost in thought. ''I promise to honor our marriage vows and never do anything to make you regret marrying me,'' he finally answered. ''As for the rest—'' he looked at her in a way that sent her blood racing ''—I'll leave that up to you. But I can promise you I'll never ask more of you than you're ready to give.''

She wanted to turn him down, to tell him she could take care of herself, but Carly's smiling face flashed before her eyes. Maybe she was wrong to want another romantic marriage. Her daughter's welfare was more important than her fantasies. Maybe she was wrong to want anything more than the protection of Tom's name.

She had to believe there was someone up there watching over her and Carly.

Mentally murmuring a silent prayer, she nodded.

''Is that supposed to be a yes?''

"Yes," she whispered, "I'll marry you."

His face broke into a broad smile, but her decision brought her new fears with it. "What if it occurs to the girls to wonder why we're getting married when we just met such a short time ago? What if they ask, what would we tell them?"

"Little girls love fairy tales—I've had the chance to learn that much," he answered. "We can make up a romantic story."

"You're right." She met his eyes and let go of her own romantic dreams. "Carly loves fairy tales."

"I'm glad you said yes." As if he wanted to say something more, the soft expression that came over his face when she'd agreed to marry him faded.

"Now, if it's all right with you," he said briskly, "I think we should get married as soon as school is out the end of the week. I'd like to have the ceremony at the convalescent home where my mother is staying. It would mean a lot to her."

Laura didn't care where they were married, not when it felt as if theirs wasn't going to be a real marriage. "Of course, but don't you think we ought to talk to the girls first?"

"I don't know about Carly, but I know Beth will be tickled to have her in the family. As a matter of fact—" he grinned "—she's already told my mother that Carly is her twin."

Laura froze. In the stress of trying to decide to accept Tom's marriage proposal, she'd forgotten the possibility that Carly wasn't her biological daughter—that she could have been her surrogate mother.

She knew there may have been a time when any issues of parenthood of test-tube babies could have been handled quietly, but not now. The rumors of the clinic's misappropriation of embryos, the availability of DNA evidence and the public fascination with the story had ended any chance of privacy.

What if Carly discovered there was a chance Tom was her biological father?

Or that Jody could be her biological mother and might actually try to take her away, or even to share her custody?

What if Jody prevailed?

As if she'd spoken her fears out loud, Tom spoke.

"I don't think we have to worry about Jody right now, but, as I said before, I think we ought to stay one step ahead of her. And if and when the time comes, I know of a few ways to keep things under wraps."

His obvious sincerity filled her with reluctant gratitude. She hadn't felt she could trust him before, but maybe she could trust him now.

"One thing more," he said, looking at her expectantly. "We have to decide where we're going to live. Your place or mine?"

Laura was struck dumb. She'd been so upset by Tom's unexpected proposal, she hadn't thought that far ahead.

Carly's room had twin beds, Beth could move in there. But what would everyone think if it somehow came out she and Tom had separate rooms? They might know the marriage was a sham.

Visions of Tom sharing her bedroom, hanging his clothing in her closet and his toothbrush next to hers flashed in front of her eyes. What would she do if he actually expected to share her bed?

Tom's voice broke into her tumbling thoughts. "We have to live together to make it look real, you know, or the marriage wouldn't hold water."

Which brought Laura back to her unanswered question: How much of a marriage would their marriage be?

"Live together?" she echoed. "What is that supposed to mean?"

"Come on, Laura," he answered impatiently. "We're both adults. We ought to be able to share a home, or a bed for that matter, without behaving like kids."

Gazing at Tom's very masculine body and feeling her growing reaction to him, Laura had no doubts they were both adults. It had been that realization and the effect it was having on her that was unsettling her.

"I have to know just what this marriage entails before we go any further," she repeated, brushing her hair away from her cheek with a hand where bits of cookie dough lingered.

Tom studied the rosy hue on Laura's face, the embarrassment evident in her eyes and in her body language. And the new smudge of cookie dough on her cheek.

"Only what you want it to entail," he finally answered, more to remind himself than for her sake. If he had his way, they'd be really and truly married.

He told himself he'd had enough. He'd promised Laura his name and his protection—what else did she expect of him? To behave like a saint?

Judging from the blush on her face, it looked as if she expected him to hop into bed with her from day one. She was wrong. He could damn well control his libido any time he wanted to. Not that he wanted to— he had to.

She was off-limits until she trusted him, he told himself. But he sure as hell was going to have a problem if she didn't stop reminding him they'd soon be man and wife.

"I guess that Beth and I could move in here with you. I can leave my place for my mother." What he hadn't planned on was what their relationship would be once he and Beth had moved in.

He finally understood the blush on Laura's face, and why his own blood was suddenly running hot. It looked as if living together meant a whole new set of rules to live by.

It was too late to discuss any intimate details now, not without looking like a fool. But he guessed the time would come pretty soon when they'd have to.

"You're right," she answered, the blush on her face growing deeper as she spoke. "If you're willing to take things one day at a time, so am I. We can live here. Go ahead and make the wedding plans. In the meantime, I'll have to think of a way to break the news to the girls and my sister, Dina. She and her family are the only family I have."

Tom shared her frustration. Explaining the marriage to the girls was going to be easy. But explaining it to anyone else who knew them was another story.

"I'd like you to meet my mother," he said. "And while we're there, I can make all the arrangements for the wedding with the home's director. Would tomorrow after we drop the girls at school be too soon?"

TOM LED THE WAY to the home's day room. He found his mother seated in a wheelchair in front of a large bay window enjoying a few fleeting rays of sunshine before a threatening storm broke.

"Hi, Mom! Glad to see you out of bed and looking good!"

Smiling happily, Alicia Aldrich welcomed Tom with a kiss. "I do feel much better," she replied. "In fact, you don't look so bad yourself. Thank heavens you look a lot better than you did the other day."

"That's because I've managed to solve a problem or two," he answered. "With a little help, that is." He drew Laura to his side. "Mom, I'd like you to meet Laura Edwards. Laura, my mother, Alicia."

"I'm pleased to meet you, Laura," his mother answered with an inquiring glance at Tom. "Are you the 'little help' my son is talking about?"

"Yes, I suppose I am." Laura eyed Tom helplessly. His eyes warned caution.

Alicia Aldrich patted the empty chair beside her wheelchair. "Come over and sit here by me, dear, and tell me how you managed to put a smile on my son's face."

Laura felt like a hypocrite. How much of the facts did Tom's mother already know? How much of the true story about the reasons for her being here could she safely reveal?

Even to Laura, the facts seemed bizarre. To anyone else, they were sure to sound downright foolish. To Tom's mother, who obviously loved him, they might sound even worse. Not that she could blame her. If she wasn't living the charade, she would never have believed it herself.

When Laura hesitated, Alicia spoke. "Tell me," she said quietly, "by any chance are you the mother of a little girl named Carly?"

"Why, yes, I am," Laura replied. "How did you know?"

A wry smile, so like Tom's, crossed his mother's face. "Tom told me a little about the problems surrounding the girls, and you, too. I take it you're part of the solution?"

"Laura *is* the solution, Mom," Tom answered. He touched Laura's shoulder with an affectionate gesture Laura felt was designed to make his mother believe they cared for each other. "I've asked her to marry me and she's accepted."

The smile faded from his mother's face.

"I understand the two of you have known each other for only a little while. Are you sure you want to do this, my dear?"

When Laura remained silent, her future mother-in-law gazed inquiringly at her son.

"I don't know exactly what you and my son have in mind, but I don't think it would be fair for either of you to enter into a marriage unless you care for each other."

Tom's eyes challenged Laura.

Laura wanted to tell his mother the truth. Telling a lie—even a white lie designed to keep Alicia Aldrich from worrying—was foreign to her nature. She wanted to tell her that, thrown together by mutual need, she and Tom were marrying in order to form a family to protect their daughters from his ex-wife. And that only the future would show if the attraction between them would grow into something more.

And to hope she'd understand that if there had been any other way for them to keep their children out of harm's way, Tom would have found it.

"Mrs. Aldrich, the fact is…" Her voice broke off when Tom's hand tensed on her shoulder.

Laura didn't know if he meant it as a warning, but from the plea in his eyes, she realized he was asking her to back him up.

"You don't have to worry about us, Mrs. Aldrich," Laura stated. "I wouldn't have consented to marry Tom if I hadn't wanted to."

"Well, that sounds more like a prospective new-lywed," Tom's mother answered. "Now that that's settled, why don't you call me Alicia?" She smiled happily when Laura agreed. "You'll have to forgive me, my dear. I only have your welfare in mind." She beamed up at Tom. "Why don't you give Laura a big kiss?"

Tom glanced around him. Small clusters of patients with curious eyes were everywhere. "Here?"

"Of course here, so I can share in your happiness," his mother replied. "This place could do with a little livening up."

At her urging, Laura rose and went into Tom's arms. He whispered "Thank you," in her ear. "You won't be sorry, I promise."

Before she could answer, he bent his head and covered her lips with his. At first, his kiss was gentle. Until he took her head in his hands and kissed her with an urgency that sent hot waves of sensation coursing through her.

Laura sensed it was more than an ordinary kiss. That the look in his eyes spoke of more than gratitude. The pressure of his lips, the strength in his arms as he pressed her to his muscular body, spoke of more than a token embrace. He wanted her, and heaven help her, she wanted him.

She hadn't planned on this, Laura thought dimly through a haze of desire. He was going too far, too fast. Hadn't they already agreed that theirs was going to be a marriage of convenience? Surely, he didn't expect her to be a real bride? She trembled in his arms.

As if sensing her reaction, he abruptly let her go.

"Now that that's settled," Alicia Aldrich said with a happy sigh, "where and when do you plan this wedding?"

"We've decided to get married here next weekend, Mom, so you can attend the wedding."

"I'd like nothing better." She beamed at Laura. "It looks as if I'm not only going to get a daughter, I'm also going to get another grandchild to love. And, from the looks of things, maybe a few more!"

Laura's heart took a dive.

Chapter Nine

As far as providing new grandchildren for her pro-spective mother-in-law to love, Laura wasn't all that sure her marriage to Tom was likely to produce any more babies. More than ever, Laura needed to talk over her pending unorthodox marriage with her sister.

Now that her romantic dreams were shattered, she needed the pragmatic Dina to tell her if she was doing the right thing by marrying Tom.

"Now that I've met your mother, I'd like you to meet my sister, Dina, and her family," she told Tom on the way home.

"Sure," Tom answered, carefully steering his way through the sluggish afternoon traffic, complicated by the darkening skies. As the month of December wore on and daylight hours grew shorter, so did motorists' tempers, including his own. "Better make it soon. While you were visiting with Mom, I arranged to have our wedding next weekend."

Laura felt herself blanch.

He glanced her way. "You haven't changed your mind, have you?"

"No, it's just that I haven't had much time to think about marriage."

He took his right hand off the steering wheel and gently squeezed her knee in sympathy. "There isn't any time to think about it. Relax, everything is going to be okay."

If he meant to reassure her she had nothing to worry about, he was going about it in the wrong way. Not with the pressure of his hand heightening her sexual awareness of him and her bewildering reaction to it.

"I know just how you must feel," he said with a thoughtful smile. He put his hand back on the steering wheel. "Tell me, do you know how to swim?"

"Yes, I can swim if I have to. But what does swimming have to do with our getting married?"

"Just this. Pretend you're about to dive into deep water. Just hold your breath and jump."

Laura glanced at his profile, where a smile hovered at the corner of his lips. Jump? Jump where? At visions of jumping and landing in his arms, of being kissed with those full, sensuous lips, of his muscular body cradling her against him, she laughed nervously. "That's quite an analogy, but maybe you're right. But I'd still like to call Dina when I get home and ask if we can all come over tomorrow night. I'd like her to meet you."

"Think she'll approve of our getting married?" Tom asked as he pulled to a stop at an intersection.

Laura glanced sharply at him. His self-assurance seemed to have slipped a notch or two since she'd mentioned her sister.

"Why not?" she asked. "Is there something about you that you're afraid people won't like?"

"Not at all," he answered. "It's just that I spend so much of my time working undercover as an immigration agent, I don't get to know many people—the right kind of people, that is. And sometimes," he added with a quick, rueful glance in her direction, "I'm not always sure if I'm as civilized as I ought to be."

If he had been facing her, she was sure there would have been a wicked, suggestive grin on his face. Civilized? Where? At a dinner table? In bed? Thank goodness the signal changed and Tom turned his attention to the road. Now she could get back to talking about a more practical and a less arousing subject: their visit to her sister.

"I don't think you have anything to worry about on that score. I'll simply introduce you as the man I plan to marry. I'm sure Dina and Jeb will make you feel right at home."

Laura knew it had taken a lot of courage for Tom to confess, even as a joke, that he wasn't sure her sister might approve of him. She saw a frown pass over his forehead. He was more human and vulnerable than he'd let on. And, it seemed, so was she.

Was he still strong enough to stand between her and Jody's threats?

ON THE WAY to school the next morning, Tom picked up Laura and Carly. With the girls happily giggling in the back seat, he exchanged glances with Laura. "Who's going to tell the little ladies we're getting married—you or me?"

Married! Laura felt an excitement run through her. Until now, her agreement to marry a man she was both highly attracted to and felt was a danger to her at the same time hadn't seemed real. Her head reminded herself the marriage was nothing more than a convenience. So why did her body heat up whenever their eyes met? Who was she fooling?

"I will," she answered. "I think I can tell them in a way little girls understand."

"Be my guest." He raised an eyebrow. "Maybe it will answer some of my questions, too."

Laura felt herself color. "What questions? I thought we had an agreement."

"Go ahead," he answered with a grin. "I'll let you know when the time comes."

Since she no longer was sure she had all the answers, Laura wasn't sure she was looking forward to his questions. "I'll tell the girls when we get to the school."

"Good enough." He winked.

She blushed.

When they arrived at school, Laura took the girls aside. "How would the two of you like to live together?"

Carly and Beth exchanged surprised glances. "Like forever?" Carly asked.

"Like forever," Laura agreed. She smiled at the growing excitement on their faces. Sadly, she knew from experience "forever" was only a moment in time.

"Would we live in your house?" Beth wanted to know.

"Yes."

"And me and Carly would have the twin beds?"

"Yes," Laura agreed again.

Beth glanced at her father. "Is my daddy going to live there, too?"

"Yes, sweetheart," Tom answered as he joined the conversation. "We're all going to live there together."

"Why, Daddy? And what about Grandma?"

"Because Carly's mother and I are going to get married. And when Grandma feels better, she'll be home waiting for you to visit."

For a moment, Beth looked stunned. She and Carly looked at each other. Then they rushed at each other and hugged. "Cool!"

LAURA'S SISTER'S HOME was a two-story Tudor of timber and stone, surrounded by a small formal garden. Built in the late thirties, it had all the stately ambience of an English country squire's home. She and Carly were frequent visitors—or had been until the events of the past two weeks had caught up with her.

A few years older than Laura, Dina Applegate bore her years with a friendly dignity that masked an intuitive mind. With three young boys and a husband who was a doctor, nothing seemed to faze her. As far as Laura was concerned, if Dina approved of Tom, she could forget her own qualms about marrying him.

When Dina greeted them in her usual friendly manner, Laura breathed a sigh of relief. In spite of her earlier telephone call telling Dina she was planning to marry a complete stranger, nothing had changed.

"Hi, I'm Laura's sister, Dina, and you must be

Tom Aldrich. The kids have been driving me crazy
ever since I told them you were coming over. They
couldn't wait to meet you. Me, too.'' She smiled.

"Thanks.'' Tom grinned. "I understand you're the
one who gives Carly all those Barbie dolls. Laura tells
me she's afraid you spoil her.''

"Not enough,'' Dina answered with a secret smile
at Carly. "With three boys of my own all involved
in heart-stopping physical activities, and a husband
who shares them, I need a real little girl to pamper.''

Dina kissed Laura on the cheek, hugged Carly and
beamed at Tom. Laura relaxed. She'd worried for
nothing. No matter how he may have felt on the inside, Tom appeared to be comfortable, outgoing and
interested in her family.

"Here, let me take your things.'' While Tom took
off his overcoat, Dina glanced behind him. "And this
little sweetheart must be Beth.''

Suddenly shy, Beth hung back until Tom took her
by the hand and introduced her. "Yes, this is Beth. I
call her pumpkin.''

"Daddy!''

"That's all right, sweetheart, don't let your father's
teasing bother you,'' Dina said as she helped Beth
take off her coat. She leaned down and whispered
loudly in Beth's ear, "Just remember, little boys are
born to tease. But they only tease girls they like.''

Beth giggled. "Daddy's not a little boy.''

Dina straightened, glanced at Tom, then met
Laura's eyes with a smile. "No, he's not, is he?''

Laura took a good look at Tom. The fact that he
would become her husband in a few short days suddenly took on a new dimension. In twill slacks, choc-

olate-brown jacket and a beige wool turtleneck sweater, Tom was six feet of pure adult male from the top of his golden-brown hair to his tan half boots. And judging by the widening smile on her sister's face, his magnetic smile was catching.

Laura tried to see him through her sister's eyes. He looked and acted like any well-bred man. And in spite of his easygoing manner, he looked sincere. No wonder Dina appeared to be pleased. But she could tell from the side glances Dina was sending her that she still had dozens of questions to ask.

"My sister is right, with three young boys, she knows just how they think," she told Beth. "Carly has learned to take their teasing, and to tease back. I know you will, too."

Tom relaxed at the friendly repartee. When Jeb came into the room, Tom was ready to play the part of a man in love and about to marry the woman of his dreams.

"Uncle Jeb, we're going to get married!" Carly burst out when she saw her uncle.

"You are?" he answered. He lifted her into his arms and high above his head until she squealed with delight. "And here I thought it was your mother who was getting married."

"Yes, but Beth and I are going to get married, too. Mommy says so. I'm going to have a sister! Isn't that cool?"

"Yes, that's real cool!" Jeb hugged her again and set her down beside Beth. The resemblance between the two girls was so obvious, he blinked. His smile faded and he looked at Laura questioningly.

"It's a long story," she said quietly. "Later?"

Her brother-in-law nodded. "Come on in for a drink. Carly, why don't you take Beth to meet the boys? They're in the den. It wasn't easy, but I made them agree to wait in there instead of jumping all over you. And, this time, for what it's worth, they've promised to behave. I can't promise how long that will last."

"Okay, Uncle Jeb." Carly giggled. "Come on, Beth."

When the girls were gone, Jeb turned back to Tom. "I'm Jeb, Dina's husband," he said quietly. "I take it you're part of the long story?"

At Jeb's searching look, Tom knew instinctively that he was a man who couldn't be fooled easily. It was also obvious he intended to make certain no one took advantage of Laura.

"I wasn't exactly in on the beginning of the story in person, at least not knowingly," Tom answered, returning Jeb's steady gaze, "but I'm going to do my best to give it a happy ending."

"In that case, I'm glad to see you." Jeb extended his hand for Tom to shake. "Come with me. You can tell me about the 'exactly' part of the story."

Tom smiled reassuringly when his eyes met Laura's. He'd have to take his chances, tell her brother-in-law as much of the truth as he was able and hope Jeb was still agreeable to their marriage. He didn't even want to think of what might happen if he wasn't.

Jeb led the way to the living room where a bar had been set up alongside the brick fireplace aglow with real logs. The sharp smell of the burning pine mingled with the scent of spiced apples. A partially decorated

Christmas tree stood in front of the large bay window. Boxes of ornaments were piled on the floor and soft Christmas music played in the background.

Jeb glanced at Tom. "What'll it be? Mulled apple cider, or maybe something stronger?"

"Apple cider would be fine, thank you."

Jeb poured Tom a tall mug. "Laura?"

"Laura's going to come with me and help with dinner," Dina said, urging Laura out of the room. "You two can get acquainted. I'll call when dinner is ready."

"You'll have to forgive me for not being more friendly when we were introduced," Jeb said when Dina and Laura disappeared. "But my sister-in-law has had a rough time of it since Carly's father was killed. I'm sure you understand that I want to be sure she's going to be okay with this marriage." Tom nodded.

Jeb added another log to the fire and gestured to a pair of burgundy-colored velvet armchairs close by. "Why don't you sit down and we'll talk."

"Nice place you have here," Tom commented, gazing at the comfortable room with the flowered sofa and a cherry wood coffee table and side tables. Bronze lamps reflected the glow of the fireplace. Filled bookcases covered a wall. A large family portrait of Jeb, Dina and their three boys hung over the fireplace.

"It's always nicer at Christmastime," Jeb agreed, gesturing to the large pine partially decorated Christmas tree. "We trim the tree in easy stages," he laughed. "That way it makes the season last longer. It's a family custom, although I know it drives the boys crazy. They can't wait to see their presents piled under the tree, and they can't wait to open them, either." He took the second armchair and sat back. "Now, tell me how you and Laura met."

Tom delayed his answer by taking a deep swallow of his cider. How much of the truth could he tell his prospective brother-in-law and still make his pending marriage sound like a romantic one? Two weeks ago, he hadn't met Laura, let alone planned to marry her. If he told Jeb the whole truth, the guy would sure as hell invite him outside. Not that he'd blame him.

He told Jeb a version of the truth. He had met Laura at the school and since Beth and Carly were such good friends, he and Laura had been drawn together, too. They'd decided they had so much in common that marriage had seemed the natural thing to do.

It was as close enough to the truth as he felt comfortable with. He left out the possibility he could be Carly's father. That part hadn't been proven and was still too private and intimate to talk about.

Jeb listened quietly. "Attraction isn't exactly a reason to get married. You do love each other, don't you?"

"Of course," Tom answered sheepishly. After the difficulty he had persuading Laura to marry him, how could he have forgotten something so important?

"Actually," he added, determined to be as honest as he could, "at our ages I guess it's not the kind of romantic first love you see in the movies." He saw the friendly look in Jeb's eyes change, and realized his explanation sounded cold, impersonal. "You might say it's more of the kind of love that comes with having been given a second chance."

Jeb nodded, seemingly appeased. At least, for now. "I hope you'll pardon me for asking, but just what is it that you do for a living? Dina seemed awfully vague."

"Maybe it's because no one is supposed to talk about the job," Tom answered. "I'm an agent with the INS, and my work takes me undercover a great deal."

"Immigration and Naturalization Service," Jeb murmured. "Guess you're not the most popular kid on the block, are you?"

"Maybe not," Tom answered with a wry smile. "But I like to think that I'm not only enforcing the laws of my country, but that I'm keeping a lot of innocent people from being victimized by smugglers who prey on desperate dreams."

"Hey, I didn't mean to criticize," Jeb protested. "It's just that I wouldn't want your job to put Laura and Beth in any kind of jeopardy."

"It won't," Tom answered firmly, meeting Jeb's eyes right on. "You have my word. In fact, I'd stake my life on it."

Jeb nodded and toyed with his empty mug. "It's kind of weird the way your two girls look so much alike. Don't you agree?"

Prepared for the obvious question, Tom had his answer ready.

"Laura and I haven't stopped talking about the resemblance," Tom assured him honestly. "They could be taken for twins."

"Which brings me to another question. And before I ask it, I should tell you I'm a doctor and I've seen and heard a lot of disturbing rumors about the Eden

Fertility Clinic where Laura works. I also know the circumstances of Carly's birth. Are you and Laura somehow involved in the scandal surrounding the clinic headlined in all the newspapers?''

Tom put his mug down on a small table between them. It was time for the truth and nothing but the truth. "It's not for publication," Tom said frankly, "but it looks as if we are. Although, there's nothing positive about our cases yet."

IN THE KITCHEN, Dina closed the door behind her. "Now, tell me what this is all about. You can't just call out of the blue and tell me you're going to get married. Not that I have anything against Tom, but from what you said, you haven't known him very long. You've been alone for six years, why the hurry to get married so quickly now?"

Laura hesitated. She was torn by the need to tell her sister the whole story and the need to honor Tom's request for secrecy. She had to tell the truth and make it sound as if she *wanted* to marry Tom, and not because she *needed* to marry him.

"If I tell you the reason, will you promise me you won't tell anyone, not even Jeb?"

Dina glanced at the door, then nodded. "I promise, but only because it's you, Laura. I never keep anything from Jeb, and he doesn't keep anything from me. This had better be good."

"You remember that Carly was an in vitro baby?"

"Of course." Dina smiled fondly. "And a very precious one at that."

Too precious to give up without a fight.

Laura went on to tell Dina about the way she and

Tom had met, their surprise that their daughters looked so much alike and about his coming to the fertility clinic after the story about the misappropriation of donors' sperm and egg contributions had hit the newspaper headlines. She told her about Carly's resemblance to Tom's ex-wife, but left out Jody's threats to ask for both Carly's and Beth's part-time custody—Dina would only worry. She ended with her decision to marry Tom to keep the girls together.

Dina gasped. "You're out of your mind! Wait a minute, are you telling me you both are involved in the way the clinic handled donor sperm and eggs?"

"Unfortunately, yes," Laura agreed unhappily. "It looks more and more as if we may be."

"You may be?" Dina echoed. Her gaze became horrified. "Are you saying that Tom and his ex may actually be Carly's parents?"

"That's what I'm saying," Laura murmured. "I wish I could find another way to account for Carly's resemblance to Beth, but I can't. Can you?"

"No, I guess not, not without asking Jeb." Dina looked troubled. "But Carl still could have been her biological father... Good heavens," she burst out. "If he wasn't, that would make you...what?"

"Carly's mother," Laura answered firmly. "And as of next weekend, Tom's wife."

Dina threw her arms around Laura and hugged her. "And here I was so happy for you, happy you'd found another great guy who loves you. Oh, Laura, I'm so sorry everything has worked out this way." She held Laura away from her. "But at least you love Tom, don't you?"

"I'm afraid so," Laura answered softly.

"Afraid of what, for heaven's sakes?"

"Afraid he doesn't love me."

They stood gazing at each other until Dina broke the silence. "Are you sure you still want to marry Tom? Are you asking me if you're doing the right thing?"

The kitchen door swung open before Laura could answer.

"Ready for the steaks?" Jeb headed for the indoor grill and the bowl of steaks marinating beside it.

Laura cast a warning look at her sister. Dina nodded, then answered Jeb. "Go ahead and put them on. The potatoes are ready and warming in the oven and the salad is in the refrigerator."

"You're a pair of fast ladies," Jeb laughed. "Pardon the pun." Puzzled, Jeb looked around at the lack of food preparation.

"So, what have you ladies been talking about?"

"Women's secrets," Dina said shortly.

"Oh-oh." Jeb balled his hands into clenched fists and pretended to fend Dina off. He looked helplessly at Tom. "When my wife uses that tone of voice on me, I know enough to butt out. Okay, sweetheart, I give up. What have you planned for the kids' dinner?"

"Hot dogs," Dina answered. "They hate steaks." She took a package out of the refrigerator and handed it to him. "You can put them on the grill. I have macaroni and cheese ready in the oven."

"Want me and Tom to set up tray tables in the den for the kids?"

"No, this is a family night." Her thoughtful gaze

included Tom. "We're all going to eat together and get acquainted."

"Great! Come on, Tom, tonight is a celebration. After I get the steaks on, you and I can break out a special bottle of wine."

Laura watched the friendly rapport between her brother-in-law and Tom. Jeb, like Dina, had always been a good judge of people. From the looks of things, Tom had passed with flying colors.

"CARLY SAYS you're going to be her new dad." Dina and Jeb's eldest son Steven speared him with a glance.

"That's about right," Tom answered, swallowing the last of his wine. He smiled at Steven. "Your aunt and I are getting married next weekend."

Steven glanced at his father. "Dad told us not to ask you too many questions, so I guess I better not."

"Why, what did you want to know?"

"Are you a doctor like Dad?"

"No," Tom answered as he regarded the serious fourteen-year-old boy. "You might say I work for the United States government."

"Are you a politician?"

"No, I'm not."

Steven eyed him soberly. Tom could see the wheels of thought going around in the boy's head. "You can't tell me who you are, can you?"

Tom shook his head. "I'm afraid not." He watched the speculation grow in Steven's eyes. If this kept up, the kid was bound to think he was a government spy, or some other glamorous type so popular on TV and in the movies. The last thing he wanted to be thought of was a hero.

"How about you?" he asked, relaxing in the friendly atmosphere. "What are you and your brothers into?"

This was what he'd missed—a happy family life, he thought as he listened to Steven describe the family hobbies. Maybe if he hadn't taken refuge in his career, he would have had a large family by now. Maybe Jody hadn't been all that wrong about him when she'd accused him of thinking his job was more important to him than she was. By then, he'd become so accustomed to her tirades every time he came home he'd shrugged her off. Maybe he should have listened.

He gazed thoughtfully across the table at Laura. The comment he'd made to Jeb was true. Laura *was* giving him a second chance to be a proper husband, to have a full family life. Wife, children—the whole bit. He silently vowed never to betray her trust in him.

When their gazes met, he put his heart into his smile.

The last of Laura's tension slowly vanished. If she'd had any doubts about Tom or if he would fit in with her only remaining family, they were gone. But he'd left her with another kind of tension. The kind that warmed her middle, made her heart beat faster and made her hormones stir restlessly.

Hoping Dina hadn't read the invitation in Tom's smile, or her response to it, Laura glanced quickly at her sister. Dina grinned and motioned her approval. Jeb, at the head of the table, caught her glance and signaled his own support.

For Laura, the rest of the evening passed in a happy haze and ended with promises to meet again at the wedding.

TOM GLANCED in the rearview mirror at the girls. By the time they'd driven two blocks, both were fast asleep snug in their seat belts.

"Thank you for tonight, Laura," he said. "Your sister has a great family. With Mom taking care of Beth, and me away so much of the time, I'm afraid I never realized what I was missing."

"Yes, they are wonderful," she replied, her heart more free than it had been in years. "They're the biggest reason I've been able to handle the past six years. They've always included me and Carly as a part of their family."

"And now you and I can have a family of our own," Tom said comfortably.

"We will?" Laura questioned softly.

He glanced sharply at her. "Why not? Do you have any doubts?"

"Only because we're getting married to stop Jody, for one thing. And, for another, because you keep telling me you're attracted to me."

"Don't tell me there's something wrong with my being attracted to you! I thought you'd be pleased."

"No," she answered with a wistful sigh, "but that's more of a physical response, not real love. After being married for sixteen years, Dina and Jeb are still madly in love with each other. That's what makes their marriage so perfect."

"Well," Tom answered with that grin of his that

made her heart swing to double time, ''don't write us off, yet. There's always tomorrow. Besides, the way I see it, the attraction between us is a good place to start.''

Chapter Ten

The day room of the convalescent home had been decorated with boughs of holly and vases of bright-red hollyhocks. A large crystal bowl filled with red-and-green-colored ice cubes floating in fruit punch waited on a red-and-white tablecloth. Two large plates of nonfat cookies, contributed by the bride and delivered earlier by the groom, rested beside it. Paper plates, cups and green forks and spoons made the table look festive. A Christmas tree, transferred from the lobby for the occasion, filled a corner.

The minister stood under an arch made of pine tree branches. The guests, largely in wheelchairs and dressed in their finest, were ready. The pianist softly played Christmas carols.

The only thing missing were the bride and groom.

Beth, resplendent in her long pink bridesmaid's dress and a wreath of flowers in her hair, peeked around the door where the wedding party waited to survey the scene of the wedding.

"Daddy! Hurry, everyone's waiting for us. The piano lady is playing the same music over and over again."

Carly, fidgeting in her identical bridesmaid's dress, pressed her bouquet to her chest and looked worried. "Mommy?"

"Make up your mind, Laura," Tom said in an undertone. "You're making everyone nervous. Either you're ready to get married, or you're not. You have to make up your mind."

Laura swallowed the lump in her throat and thought of Tom's suggestion she think of getting married as jumping into deep water and swimming as fast as she could.

"I do want to get married. It's just that this is so different—it doesn't feel like a wedding." She gazed around her at Alicia Aldrich's room, where they were waiting before the wedding ceremony began.

Dressed in her finery, the room's occupant was at the wedding celebration. Her room was furnished with a hospital bed covered in crisp white linen. A small table held a yellow lamp, a few family photographs and a glass with a lone flower in it. An ancient rocker with a neatly folded yellow-and-white afghan on the seat rested in the corner in front of a small television set.

"This doesn't seem real," Laura murmured.

"Oh, it's real enough," he answered, taking her by the arm and leading her to the floor-length mirror on the bathroom door. "Take a look."

She saw herself clothed in an off-white, long-sleeved lace confection with a matching halo of a lace hat on her chestnut hair. Her wedding bouquet, a gift from her prospective mother-in-law and delivered by a well-known florist, was made of delicate maidenhair fern and small red picture roses. Her face was pale.

Beside her, Tom was dressed in a navy-blue suit, a light-blue shirt and a blue-and-white striped tie. A sprig of mistletoe was pinned to a lapel.

He had never looked so virile, so handsome, so masculine.

She'd never felt so lost.

He gestured to Beth and Carly. ''Come on over here, ladies.'' When they ran over, he positioned the girls in front of Laura and himself.

''So, tell me, Mrs. Aldrich, just what do you think is missing in this picture?''

''I'm not Mrs. Aldrich yet,'' she answered faintly.

''You will be if you can get on with this,'' he answered. ''Take a good look and tell me what it is that you think is missing.''

''I guess one of the things missing is the church,'' she answered softly glancing around the room.

''But the minister isn't,'' Tom said, gently turning her face back to the mirror. ''From what I hear, he's in the next room waiting for us. Anything else?''

As if he were aware it wasn't the lack of a church that bothered her, his gaze challenged hers in the mirror. She saw herself blush.

He was right.

The truth was, she wasn't used to thinking of him as her husband. The prospect of the unresolved wedding night ahead was turning her insides into knots.

She gazed steadily at Tom's questioning eyes.

He hadn't pretended to be anything he didn't appear to be.

He'd as good as said he never intended to be her husband at all—except in name.

He'd never pretended to be in love with her.

He was a pragmatic man who'd told her they should get married in order to protect two small girls, one of them her own, and she'd agreed.

So why was she so reluctant to marry him?

Marriage should mean loving and making a home for their family, she thought unhappily. As Tom's wife, she might never know either. Could she settle for less than her heart yearned for?

"Can we go and get married now, Daddy?" Beth asked anxiously.

"Mommy? Can we go and get married now?"

When Carly echoed Beth's question, Laura decided it was too late to change her mind even if she wanted to. How could she deny Carly a living father who was more than a picture in a photo album? A father who'd already promised to protect her and keep her safe as he did his own child?

How could she deny Beth the chance for a home with a sister and a father and mother who loved her?

She met Tom's eyes in the mirror.

"Yes. Let's all go and get married."

"Do you, Thomas Aldrich, take this woman to be your lawfully wedded wife, to have and to hold, to love and to cherish, in sickness and in health from this day forward?"

"I do."

Tom smiled down at his bride, a surge of emotion sweeping through him at the thought Laura was about to become his wife: to care for, to protect, and, if good fortune was smiling at him as he hoped, to love.

The minister nodded and turned his gaze on the bride.

"Laura Edwards, do you take this man to be your lawfully wedded husband, to have and to hold, to love and to cherish, from this day forward?"

"I do," she answered softly.

"Then, by the authority vested in me by the State of California, I now pronounce you man and wife."

The minister paused and gazed benevolently at the bridal party. As if he'd left something out of the ceremony, he paused and cleared his throat.

Tom was about to prompt him with the you-may-kiss-the-bride bit when the minister glanced down at the bridesmaids' awed faces. "Ah yes," he murmured. "I remember now."

"Do you, Beth Anne, accept Laura as your mother and Carly Jane as your sister?"

"Oh yes, I do!"

"Do you, Carly Jane, accept Thomas as your father and Beth Anne as your sister?"

"I do, I do!" Carly squealed happily.

"Then," the minister continued, "by the virtue of their parents' marriage, I now pronounce Beth Anne Aldrich and Carly Jane Edwards sisters."

Tears stung at Tom's eyes when the two little bridesmaids exchanged happy grins. Glancing over at Laura, he felt a new tenderness, a deepening of an irrevocable responsibility for the three women in his life.

The minister smiled at the girls and got back to

business. "And now, Thomas, you may kiss the bride."

The wedding guests burst into applause. Carly and Beth hugged each other. The pianist enthusiastically broke into a spirited rendition of "Happy Days Are Here Again."

The kittens, who had been asleep in Alicia Aldrich's lap, awakened with a hiss, arched their backs and bared tiny teeth.

More than ready to follow the minister's instructions, Tom breathed a sigh of relief and reached for Laura.

She didn't look like a happy bride.

Underneath the lacy halo of a hat, her face was pale, her lack of color accentuated by her vibrant chestnut hair. The hand that had remained in his after he'd placed a woven gold wedding ring upon her finger, trembled.

Laura may have consented to be his wife, but her eyes reflected her lingering doubts.

Tom's euphoria vanished. After their visit to Laura's sister, he'd been so sure he'd finally convinced Laura to trust him. He'd been sure he'd finally persuaded her to believe, that although his initial reason for suggesting they marry had begun with his desire to protect her and Carly, it had turned into something more.

He'd tried to show Laura how much he actually cared for her. And how much he hoped they could be a family and live happily ever after.

He'd even dared to hope she cared enough for him to welcome him as her husband in a real marriage. Had he been mistaken?

Was it because he hadn't come right out and told her that, given half a chance, his growing affection for her might well turn into the love he already bore her?

What was love anyway? he wondered as he returned her gaze. Physical need, or the heart's desire to watch over, protect and nourish someone you respected and cared for?

Not that he wasn't a red-blooded man. He was, in spades, when it came to his new bride. He would have liked to take her in his arms, carry her away to a special place and to make her his in body as well as name. But until he could take the uncertainty out of her eyes and put a smile back on her face, he felt committed to a platonic marriage.

Hadn't she learned by now he would do anything in his power to make her happy?

When the buzz of conversation in the background grew louder, Tom gently drew Laura to him until her body settled against his. The pressure of her breasts against his chest, the warmth of her breath against his neck and her faint, sweet scent of lilacs were magic. At the same time, he was filled with regret for what might have been if they'd met and fallen in love in a more traditional way.

It could have been so different.

The hurt must have shown in his eyes.

"Somehow, under the circumstances, I feel deceitful for making those vows," she murmured. "Don't you?"

"Laura, when I promised to love, honor and to cherish you, I meant every word," he answered softly. "It might not be the kind of love you dreamed of, but I swear that I do care for you. Enough to have and to hold and protect you from this day forward just as I promised. I hope you'll grow to care for me, too.''

The color slowly returned to Laura's cheeks. A soft glow came into her eyes. Her lips parted.

Before she had a chance to speak, Len shouted. ''Hey, wait a minute! This marriage isn't legal until Tom kisses the bride!''

Beth looked anxious. ''Does that mean that Carly and I aren't sisters yet either, Daddy?''

''Sure you are, pumpkin,'' he answered without taking his eyes off Laura. *Maybe more than you know.*

Tom held Laura to him with one hand and waved Len off with the other. ''That's what I get for asking him to be my best man,'' he said under his breath. ''But he happens to be right, you know. We can talk about this later, but first we have something important to do.''

He gently brushed his knuckles across his new wife's cheek, cupped her face and turned her face up to his. ''I guess we'll have to make this legal or he'll never let me hear the last of it.''

He bent to cover Laura's parted lips with his own.

Laura closed her eyes and surrendered to Tom's embrace, to the pressure of his hand caressing the sensitive nape of her neck, and the urgency of his lips on hers. She tried to put aside her doubts about the wisdom of having married a stranger, and to savor the warmth of the kiss that was sending waves of pleasurable sensations, too long dormant, through her.

His kiss may have been meant to seal a loveless

marriage, but it was like none she'd ever known, or at least remembered. It was a kiss that surely went beyond a traditional exchange between a bride and groom and sent a yearning through her.

She found herself responding with a fervent kiss of her own. She put her heart and her soul into the embrace, along with silent promises of her own. He didn't know it, but she was promising to cherish him not only for now, but forever. Even though it wasn't a promise he expected her to keep.

She'd never told him, but her fear was that, for Tom, "from this day forward" in the wedding ceremony meant only until the day he'd be able to show her proof she'd been a surrogate mother. That she had no real claim on Carly, while he did. Would he still need her to be his wife then?

No matter how he'd tried to reassure her, she hadn't been able to convince herself that Tom intended their marriage to be more than a marriage of convenience. Or to convince herself that it would last after Jody forgot she wanted to play at being a mother again. Until this moment. The heated look in Tom's eyes and the almost desperate strength in his arms as he held her to him told her this marriage might turn out to be something other than she'd agreed to.

They'd spoken about the "something else" when he'd suggested marriage. For the life of her, she couldn't remember what they'd finally agreed upon or if they'd even come to an agreement at all. At the moment, all she could remember was that he'd told her they'd take one day at a time.

Considering how Tom's kiss sealed their marriage

vows, she was afraid the one-day-at-a-time agreement wasn't going to be good enough.

She had to make up her mind tonight just how much of a wife she was willing to be.

The possibilities, coupled with the look of desire in Tom's eyes and the flowering of sensation within her, sent a myriad of questions whirling through her mind.

When he finally let her go, she realized she actually knew so little about the real Tom Aldrich.

She knew his job. She knew he was a caring and compassionate man, liked children, and had a strong sense of duty and loyalty. All the traits that had come into play when he'd been called home in time to read the newspaper headlines and set himself to prevent a wrong.

And she knew that he was a man her body craved.

What she didn't know about him were the simple things that a wife needed to know about her husband: what were his favorite foods, outside of chocolate cookies? What were his interests? Or even, she blushed at the direction her mind was taking, what side of the bed did he like to sleep on?

What would happen if she actually fell in love with him when he didn't love her?

Still, she had married Tom. She had promised to love and to cherish him. Now she had to find some way to live with those promises.

Overcome with emotion, she swayed in Tom's arms.

His embrace tightened around her. "Laura, are you all right?"

"Yes," she answered as she tried to pull herself

together. "I'm afraid this marriage business is a bit overwhelming. Maybe we do need to talk some more."

He bent to kiss her again, this time lightly. "Later," he said. "When we're alone, we'll have all the time in the world to talk. Even get to know each other."

"Come on, it's time to celebrate!" Len grabbed Laura's hand and started to pull her after him. "To the punch bowl, madam."

"Wait a minute," Tom protested. "That's *my* bride you're stealing!"

"Sure, she is, but you'll have plenty of time with her later." Len winked. In an aside to Laura, he whispered, "Don't give me away, but I spiked the punch with some sparkling apple cider."

"You didn't!" Laura found herself laughing in spite of her tumultuous emotions. "Are you sure that's all you added?" She gestured to the dozen or so patients, some in walkers, some in wheelchairs, all with happy smiles on their faces. Her mother-in-law had been right. The patients needed something and someone to lighten up their lives.

Dina pushed her way past Len to congratulate her sister. She hugged her, held her at arm's length and looked anxiously into her eyes. "Sweetheart, you look so beautiful! Are you happy?"

"Yes," Laura answered. "I'm sorry I couldn't make you my maid of honor, but the girls—"

"Don't even think about it," Dina replied. "The ceremony was beautiful as is. Besides, I was your matron of honor at your first wedding. It was the girls' time to shine."

"Come on, you two, let's have some punch!" Len took Laura and Dina by their elbows and started off.

With a small bridesmaid clinging to each hand, Tom grinned and followed. Maybe it was to his advantage to have Len lighten the celebration. Maybe Laura would unwind enough to realize their marriage wasn't a charade and that he meant every promise he'd made to her.

When Beth and Carly dragged him over to his smiling mother, he cast a longing glance at his bride.

"Can we take our kittens now, Grandma?"

"Of course, sweetheart," her grandmother answered. "But be careful. The noise has made them nervous."

Carly asked wistfully, "Now that I'm Beth's sister, can I call you Grandma, too?"

Alicia Aldrich looked up at Tom with a proud smile and bent to kiss Carly's cheek. "Yes, of course, dear. Because that's what I am, you know. There, now that that's settled, how about you two young ladies bringing me a glass of punch?"

"Mommy made the cookies, Grandma. They're the healthy kind, so you don't have to be afraid to eat them," Beth told her.

"All the more reason to eat one, or maybe two," her grandmother agreed. "Run along now and bring them back. I can hardly wait."

"Sure, Grandma!"

"You know, alone Beth is a handful," Tom laughed. "I can't imagine how I'm going to manage now that there's two of them."

"You have a wife to help you now," his mother

answered placidly. "Between the two of you, I'm sure you'll find a way."

He had a wife now. And a family, too. Tom smiled.

Laura Edwards—no, Laura Aldrich as of ten minutes ago, he thought with a pleased smile—was the type of woman who *would* be a real wife. The apple-pie-and-cookies kind of a wife whose family and home were more important to her than the world that surrounded them.

He made up his mind to ask her if she would like to give up her job. To be there for the children after school, and for him when he came home at night. And, once he looked into changing his schedule, he intended to be there as many nights as he could manage.

To be sure, he reflected as he gazed over at the refreshment table where Laura was busy receiving congratulations, many of today's women preferred to work outside the home. That was all right with him, too. He didn't need a wife at home to make him feel like a man.

His mother interrupted his happy reflections. "Tom, why don't you join your wife? I'll be fine right here with the children and kittens. I'm sure my grand-daughters will be happy to entertain me."

"Thanks, Mom," he said gratefully. "You must have read my mind." He kissed her soft cheek and left to join Laura at the punch bowl.

His eyes on his new wife, he was stopped along the way by wedding guests offering their congratulations.

The home's director waylaid him before he managed to get very far.

"Mr. Aldrich, I'm afraid I have a bit of bad news for you."

Tom glanced hurriedly over at Laura; she looked okay. Behind him he could hear his mother and the girls laughing at the antics of the kittens.

What kind of bad news could there possibly be on such a wonderful day as this? The day he'd made Laura his wife and acquired another daughter?

"Can't it wait?" he answered. "I was about to join my wife."

"That's what I wanted to talk to you about," the man said with an uneasy glance around them. He lowered his voice. "There's a woman in my office who claims to be Mrs. Aldrich. She wanted to join the wedding celebration, but I didn't feel that I could allow her to come in here without your consent."

"What does she look like?" Tom asked, his good humor going south in a hurry. If the description fit, and he knew damn well it would, the woman had to be Jody. The director had been right—Jody was bad news.

"Strangely enough," the director said, darting a glance in Carly and Beth's direction, "what with her curly auburn hair, she looks like she's a relative of the children."

What was Jody doing here? What did she want? How had she known about the wedding in the first place?

"I'll go talk to her and see what she wants," Tom answered. He thanked the messenger of the bad news and, with a last lingering glance at Laura, he left for the man's office.

His fears were realized as soon as he came through

the office door. The woman studying a painting on the wall *was* Jody. Today, of all days.

He closed the office door behind him and strode into the room. "What are you doing here?"

"Goodness, don't you ever get tired of asking me that question?" she answered.

The evident annoyance on her face reminded him of the old Jody. No matter what he said, she was going to be a problem until she got what she came for.

"No. And if you didn't keep showing up, I wouldn't have to," he said bluntly into her frown. "How did you know I was getting married here to-day?"

"Simple," she said airily. "I called your old office telephone number. One of the secretaries bubbled over with the information when I told her I was a relative of yours from out of town." She paused and looked amused. "She was so enchanted with this sud-den romantic marriage of yours, she couldn't wait to give me all the details."

He ignored the sarcasm in her voice. He'd learned the hard way not to be drawn into a no-win argument with her. "Out with it, why are you here?"

"Where else would I be when my former husband takes himself a new wife?" she answered, moving around the room, picking up and putting down mag-azines. "I wanted to talk to Laura—that *is* her name, isn't it?—about Beth. After all as Beth's mother, I'm naturally concerned with my daughter's welfare."

Tom smothered a bitter laugh.

"If that's all that's worrying you, you can put your concern to rest. I assure you Laura is a fine woman

and a good mother.'' Jody wasn't concerned about
the kind of care Laura would give Beth. She had
something more devious on her mind.

''I'm sure she is, but I'd feel better speaking to her
myself,'' Jody insisted. She paused in her pacing, her
expression hardened. ''As a matter of fact, I'd prefer
to do that now.''

Tom finally realized what she wanted was a face-
to-face meeting with Laura. And that she was here to
have Laura take a good look at her. He smiled bitterly. Jody's motives were transparent. She'd finally
connected Carly's appearance to her own, and intended to impress Laura with their resemblance.

Over his dead body.

''Sorry,'' he answered, an edge in his voice meant
to intimidate. ''I wouldn't want to ruin Laura's wedding day. You'll have to make it some other time.''

Jody frowned at him for a long moment before she
shrugged. The finality in his voice must have gotten
through to her. ''In that case, I'll run along—for now.
But don't think I won't be back.'' She waited for him
to comment, but he managed to keep his temper.
''See you later.''

His skin cold at the blatant threat in Jody's voice,
Tom gazed at the empty doorway. She hadn't given
up, not the Jody he knew too well. Unless he found
a way to keep them out of her reach, she wouldn't
stop until she came face-to-face with Laura and Carly.

''Tom?'' Laura appeared in the doorway. ''Mr.
Landis told me you were in here. Is everything all
right?''

Tom made himself a promise to tell the director
what he thought of him for sending Laura after him.

Thank God he'd at least waited until Jody was out of the way!

"Everything is fine," he answered. Hoping Laura couldn't read his mind, he forced a smile on his face. "Just taking a phone call from the office."

"Oh?" She gazed around the room before her gaze settled on him. "I was sure the director said we had a visitor. Who was it?"

"You must have misunderstood him," Tom answered. "It was a phone call, and I've taken care of it."

From the look in his eyes and the tone of his voice, Laura wasn't convinced Tom was telling her the truth. Was he in some kind of danger he wouldn't tell her about? She was his wife now. Surely, he could confide in her.

She glanced around the office. A large leather couch filled one wall with a long glass-topped coffee table in front of it. Two leather chairs sat in front of a large executive desk. Paintings hung on the walls, and potted plants were placed by the door. Magazines were scattered across the top of the coffee table as if someone had been waiting in here.

It was as good a place as any to tell him she expected him to be truthful with her, now and in the future. Whatever had been important enough to take him away from their wedding celebration, she should be told.

"I think we should talk about this now," she said. "We won't have much private time once we get home."

Tom seemed to listen absently, his gaze fixed on

the office doorway. Prickles of apprehension swept over Laura. Someone *had* been in here with him.

She sank into a leather armchair. "There was someone here with you, wasn't there?"

Tom swung around to face her. "I told you, I came in here to take a telephone call."

"I don't think I can believe you," she answered, meeting his eyes. If he could lie to her about this, what else had he lied about?

"Laura," he said, rubbing the back of his neck, "I honestly don't think this is the time nor the place for this discussion."

She twisted the shiny golden wedding ring on her finger. "When is a good time for the truth between a husband and his wife?"

"Why don't you wait to discuss this when we get home? We have my mother and your sister and her family outside waiting for us," he answered. "The girls are bound to be exhausted after a day like today. We can put them to bed early, and, if you still want to, we can discuss this then."

Laura wanted to insist, but maybe he was right. Maybe this was the wrong time and place. "All right, we'll talk later," she answered reluctantly, and started for the door. "I suppose we should get back to the party before we're missed."

"Laura, wait a minute," Tom called her back. "There *is* something important I forgot to ask you."

She turned back. He was smiling at her, but she had the uncomfortable feeling his mind was still somewhere else. "What is it?"

"Our honeymoon."

Laura felt bewildered. She hadn't thought of a honeymoon, at least not theirs. Honeymoons were for lovers, certainly not for two people who'd married for convenience.

"Our honeymoon? You've never mentioned a honeymoon before now."

"I know, and I'm sorry," he apologized. "Things have moved too fast. In all the excitement of making the wedding arrangements, I simply forgot to ask you about it. Anyway, how would you like to go up to the mountain cabin for a honeymoon?"

The lopsided grin that came over his face was one of the things about him she'd fallen in love with. Too bad, this time she couldn't believe it was real.

"With the girls?"

"Of course with the girls," he agreed. "I wouldn't want to leave them alone at a time like this."

Laura caught her breath. "What do you mean, at a time like this?"

All her instincts told her she was right, he had had a visitor, someone who presented a threat. And if he wasn't the one who was in danger, it had to be Carly! She searched his face for a clue. "Has something happened I should know about?"

"Not really," he answered carefully, too carefully. "I just realized that school vacation is starting tomorrow and that you might enjoy getting away for a while. Actually, I'd already made plans to go up to the mountains for the holidays, remember?"

"I remember, but I don't believe you included a honeymoon in your plans. It sounds more as if you're planning to run away from something or someone."

"Come on, Laura," he said impatiently. "You have to trust me sooner or later. This is no way to start a marriage. I'm only talking about a honey-moon.''

''You've got it backward, haven't you?'' Laura answered, her voice rising. ''Don't you think that honesty between us should come before a honeymoon?''

She couldn't recognize herself as the indignant woman she'd become. And, from the startled look that came over her new husband's face he didn't recognize her, either.

Anger *was* unlike her, but she was tired of being manipulated, put off with sweet promises and, yes, even with the kisses that turned her blood to molten liquid.

''I've gotten along without a man in my life for more than six years, and I did fine by myself,'' she said. ''I'm not about to allow you to lie to me to protect me, if that's what you think you're doing. If your visitor concerns me or Carly, I have the right to know.''

Tom returned Laura's determined gaze with one of his own. He couldn't tell Laura about Jody's unwelcome visit. After today, he figured she'd had enough stress in the past two weeks to last her a lifetime. He'd sworn to cherish her, and in his book that meant protecting her. Even from himself.

With Jody out of the way for now, what good would it have done to tell Laura about her threats anyway?

Just as he'd had each time he'd managed to upset Laura, he wanted to take her in his arms, comfort her and kiss her fears away. To tell her how much he cared for her and that he had never lied to her and wasn't about to start now. Except to keep anyone from hurting her.

Laura backed away before he could touch her. Her look told him this was one time when he wasn't going to be able to persuade her with a kiss.

Chapter Eleven

"Thank you for making Carly my sister, Daddy," Beth whispered when Tom bent to kiss her good-night. "And for making Laura my other mommy. I like this one a lot."

"I do too, pumpkin," he answered, not surprised to find he cared for Laura more than he'd ever dreamed he would. And that he'd fallen in love with her.

"Carly, too?"

"You bet, especially Carly," he answered with a tender smile as he glanced over at his new daughter asleep in the other bed. Carly had been half-asleep when Laura had kissed her good-night and tucked her into bed. "It's been a busy day for the both of you. Now, close your eyes and go to sleep."

"Night, Daddy," Beth answered drowsily. She burrowed her way into her pillow with her kitten in her arms and fell asleep as soon as her eyes closed. Button's tiny nose and unblinking eyes stared up at him as if daring him to remove her. He didn't have the heart.

He tucked the blankets closer around Beth and

gazed in wonder at the two little girls. The probability that Carly might actually be his daughter filled him with awe. The way he felt about the doctors at Eden Clinic who had had a hand in her conception and birth was another story.

Surely the doctors must have known identical twins were halves of one whole personality. How could they have been so cruel as to deliberately separate siblings and give one to be raised by strangers?

Thank God, it was Laura who had been given Carly to carry, nurture and love.

The remarkable thing about it all was that the girls were so much alike in spite of having been raised apart. Not only in their appearance, their smiles, but in the way they seemed to understand and commune with each other.

He smiled to himself at the thought of their delight in finding each other. Now the girls would be able to grow up together as nature surely had intended.

Before he turned to leave, he cast a last lingering look at the children. Each had a tiny sleeping kitten curled in her arms. The miniature red-and-white rose nosegays they'd carried at the wedding ceremony were on the nightstand. With bits of flowers still in the auburn hair curling around their small faces still flushed with excitement, they looked like angels in a Botticelli painting.

He closed the bedroom door behind him and smothered a yawn as fatigue caught up with him. Un-buttoning his shirt collar, he took off his tie and walked down the hall to the bedroom he would share with Laura—at least until everyone's interest in their marriage was over. And for the rest of their lives, if he was able to persuade Laura they belonged together.

After his earlier experience, he'd been left with a distrust of marriage. Sure, he'd had his share of relationships, but none that had tempted him to make them permanent. Not until he'd met Laura, a woman he was already learning to love and who might some day learn to love him. A woman who was a port in the storm of his complicated life.

It was then that the reality of today's events finally hit him.

He paused at the bedroom door.

In the short space of less than two weeks, he'd met Laura and persuaded her to marry him. A beautiful woman who, until then, had been a complete stranger to him.

He'd acquired a second daughter who was in all probability his biological child, or at least, Beth's half sister.

To top off the mind-boggling series of events, Laura was waiting for him in the bedroom. The only problem was she had yet to tell him if their marriage would be consummated. After their confrontation this afternoon, he wasn't all that sure it was going to be.

Because of Laura's physical reaction after their wedding ceremony, he'd chosen not to tell her Jody had come to the convalescent home. He'd told a white lie for her own good. He hadn't counted on Laura being able to see through him.

He'd never been a praying man, but he was one now.

Tom sighed, took a deep breath, and said a silent

prayer to whichever saint it was who watched over new husbands.

He knocked softly at the bedroom door and waited until he heard Laura answer before he entered. She was curled up in a rocking chair, a blue-and-white afghan covering her to her chin.

One look was enough to tell him she was still upset with him. Her expression was determined, her lips pale. Her hazel eyes, as she regarded him, were troubled.

"Laura?" he said tentatively as he came into the bedroom. "Are you going to be all right with this? Would you rather I slept somewhere else?"

"No," she answered softly, "you can stay."

Tom's heart took a leap in his chest.

He wanted to take her in his arms and show her how much he'd changed from the cynical marriage-stung man he'd been before he'd met her. That he not only desired her as a man desires a woman, he'd fallen in love with her magical smile, her spirit. He'd wanted her from the first time he'd seen her, and he wanted her now more than ever.

He hesitated for a moment, then sat down on the edge of the bed he hoped to share with her.

The bed was covered with a blue bedspread covered with tiny yellow-and-white flowers. Matching curtains were at the windows. A nightstand held an antique brass lamp and two well-read books. Hand-hooked rugs were on the polished wooden floor.

The contrast between the cozy bedroom and Laura's cool demeanor was striking. He knew her heart was as warm as a summer's sun or she would never have surrounded herself with a setting like this.

Now he had to find a way to her heart.

"Laura?" he asked again, this time without the words he couldn't bring himself to say. Not until she indicated she was interested in hearing them and because he couldn't bear the idea he might make a fool of himself.

Laura brought her thoughts back from the cold place her mind had taken her. That Tom was waiting for her to make the next move, as he'd promised, wasn't lost on her. Nor was the realization he could soon be sleeping beside her in the bed.

She'd lived with empty days and nights for more than six years. Though she'd dated occasionally, she'd never considered marrying again because she couldn't bear the thought of losing a man she loved for the second time. But Tom was different. She wanted him for her husband for as long as fate would allow.

The longing for his strong arms to hold her, for his kiss and caress, overwhelmed her. She ached to have him bring to full flame the sexual excitement growing within her. To have him make her his in all the ways his dark eyes promised.

She searched Tom's face, his clear brown eyes. Everything about him seemed to be reaching out to her, asking her to become his wife.

"Laura, what have you decided?"

Tom's eyes spoke of heat and desire held down by rigid control. From the way he said her name, she realized he thought her silence was a rejection. She had to make up her mind now or the tenuous moment that could fill her empty heart could be lost.

She pushed the afghan to the floor and took a step

toward him. His eyes darkened with pleasure and desire as he reached for her. She came into his arms and heard his sigh of relief.

Through the sensuous texture of the blue satin bridal nightgown brushing across her breasts, she could feel the strong beat of his heart against hers. His arms crushed her to him with a hint of desperation.

"Are you sure?" he asked against her lips.

How could she explain herself and her decision when she longed for his loving? When she ached to feel his warm flesh against hers? To have him cradle her in his arms while they fulfilled their marriage vow to love and to cherish each other? How could she tell him she wanted to wait?

She had to be honest with herself, with him, even though she might break both their hearts.

"Tom," she murmured, "we're almost strangers. I hardly know you. I need time to get used to having you in my life. I have to get used to thinking of you as my husband, and of myself as your wife. We have to get to know more about each other."

He stiffened, drew back and stared into her eyes. "What do you mean, get used to being my wife? After this afternoon, I thought you already are."

"But not in all the ways that count." She had to make him understand her doubts, her fears. "I need time. I want us to live together until I can see the marriage is going to last and I'm sure we're doing the right thing. For both our sakes."

Passion slowly faded from his eyes as he studied her. "What makes you think our marriage isn't going to last?"

"For all the reasons you gave me when you suggested I could marry you in order to keep Carly."

"I must have been a damn fool," he said with a rueful smile. "I'd already grown to love you, but I was afraid you'd never believe me, considering everything you'd gone through. But that was then, this is now."

"I know," Laura answered. "But still—"

He stopped her with a gentle finger against her lips. "Isn't there anything I can say to make you believe this marriage is right?"

She shook her head.

"Then I guess if you need time for me to convince you this marriage of ours is real, I'll have to give it to you," he finally said. "How much time?"

"I'm not sure. But I also want an agreement from you."

His eyes narrowed. She could sense, almost feel, the effort it took him to take his arms away from around her. Her heart ached for him, for herself and for lost moments of loving. But she needed to have an understanding between them before the night was over, or there would be no real future for them.

"Since you don't want to tell me what went on this afternoon, I won't ask you again." She hesitated, then plunged on. If she wanted only the truth between them from now on, she had to make that clear. "But I want you to promise me that from now on you won't hide anything from me and that you'll treat me as an equal in this marriage. Even if you think you're doing it for my benefit. And I'm willing to make you the same promise."

"You're not making this marriage easy, are you?"

he said. Frustrated, he ran his fingers through his hair.
A lock of hair fell back over his forehead as soon as
he dropped his hand. "The way I see it, it's my job
as your husband to take care of you, to watch over
you, and the children, too."

"And it's my job as your wife to help you do it,"
she answered. "A successful marriage has to be a
partnership between equals."

"Be sensible, Laura," he protested, reaching for
her then pulling back. "There may be times when I
have to take care of problems myself and I—"

She interrupted him before he could finish his sen-
tence. "I never thought working at a marriage was
easy. But I have to be able to trust you'll include me
in all the things that concern me."

"Okay, if that's what you want," he finally agreed.
"Do you want me to put that in writing or is my word
enough?"

She waved the quip away. "Your promise is
enough. I'll never ask anything more of you."

"And tonight?" he said with a regretful glance at
the bed.

"I'm willing to sleep in the same bed with you
tonight and every night, if that's what you want," she
answered with a shy smile. A warmth filled her at the
thought of Tom sleeping beside her, and some day
making love to her. "And, in time…"

He shrugged, and smiled at her in that wry way of
his that never failed to catch at her heart. "Laura, you
don't want a husband, you want a saint."

"Maybe, but I have faith that everything will work
out in the end."

"In that case," he replied with a rueful grin, "I

suppose I'll have to promise to treat you as an equal partner and let you get used to having me around. Just don't expect me to reform overnight.''

''Thank you.'' Laura wanted to kiss him to show her gratitude, but decided it might not be wise to push them both too hard. Not when just the touch of his hand stirred her desire for him. It was going to be difficult enough for them to think of each other only as friends without tempting him—or herself.

''In the meantime, I guess we'd better try to get some sleep. We've had a busy day and if Carly is anything like Beth, we'll have to be up early.''

''Right.'' He shrugged off his coat and started to unbutton his shirt.

He paused and gazed at her as if he could see the blush that was rising through her. ''On the other hand, maybe I'll undress in the bathroom.''

He rummaged in the dresser drawer where he'd put a few of his things and took out a new pair of pajamas.

''Are you going to be okay?'' he asked as he paused with his shirt half off his shoulders.

She'd seen him without a shirt before, but the sight of him half undressed in her bedroom with a turned-down bed waiting for them turned her insides to jelly. She had to look away before he could read her thoughts and take her straight to bed.

''I'm fine.'' She busied herself folding the afghan and laying it across the foot of the bed. ''In case it gets any colder tonight.''

''In which case, just let me know,'' he said with a broad grin. ''I'm at your service.''

''Tom!'' She felt herself blush.

"What's the matter with that offer?" he questioned with another wicked grin. "Warming a wife is a legitimate part of a husband's duties, isn't it? And," he added thoughtfully, "now that I think about it, so is scratching her back. Right?"

Laura had to laugh. "Yes, I suppose those are a few of the things a husband can do."

"Only a few of the things?" He looked interested. "Care to fill me in about some of the other things this husband of yours will be allowed to do?"

Laura couldn't stop blushing as she returned Tom's teasing gaze. At the rate this conversation was going, she was afraid he'd have her in bed and be making love to her before she knew what hit her. She also knew she would be thrilled if he did. "Go on, get ready for bed. It's getting late and I'm tired."

Tom paused at the bathroom door. "You *will* be here when I get back?"

If he was trying to break the tension between them by teasing her, it wasn't working. She was so aware of him, every nerve in her body was sending urgent signals. "Yes, I'll be here," she answered with a smile.

She heard him turn the shower on and the shower door close. Visions of him standing nude under a torrent of water cascading down his broad shoulders and muscular chest were almost too much for her to think about. When he began to whistle an offbeat tune, she had to fight the desire to join him and make love while the water rushed over them.

She was in bed with the covers drawn to her chin when Tom came out of the steamy bathroom wearing new pajamas that still had creases. The scent of soap, hot water and aftershave lotion clung to him. As he approached the bed, she hurriedly dimmed the light and envisioned what he usually wore to bed. The answer shocked and thrilled her.

He paused at the foot of the bed and studied her. "Mind if I take the right side of the bed?"

"No, not at all. Actually, I don't have a preference." She scooted to the other side of the bed, thankful that for her peace of mind he was wearing pajamas, both top and bottoms. But the uncomfortable way he carried himself told her he usually slept without them.

His face still thoughtful, Tom slid under the covers. "Got any more pillows?"

She shoved a pillow at him and gritted her teeth. What else would he think of to make her aware of his presence? As if she needed a reminder with him close enough she could feel the heat of his body radiating through his pajamas. "Anything else?"

"Nothing you'd care to hear," he mumbled, thumping his pillows.

Laura smothered a laugh. "Good, then we can go to sleep. Good night."

She turned off the lamp and turned on her side. There was always tomorrow to look forward to, she comforted herself. A tomorrow when she would be more sure of herself and able to lose herself in his arms.

Tom lay quietly in the spot Laura had warmed for him and waited an eternity for her even breathing to tell him she'd fallen asleep. Sure as hell, *he* wasn't going to get much sleep tonight.

To add to his misery, Laura's lilac perfume drifted

across the narrow space between them. The new pajamas he'd bought and had hoped he wouldn't have to use were tight in all the wrong places and damned uncomfortable. So was his unrequited desire for his wife.

In spite of agreeing to wait until Laura became used to having him in her life, his body stirred. And his conscience, too.

Restless, he turned on his side to find that Laura had turned over in her sleep and they were practically nose to nose. Her face was flushed, a half smile on her face as she murmured in her sleep. Her proximity and her slender outline beneath the covers was tantalizing and inviting. She was smaller and more delicate than he'd imagined her to be. Idly, he wondered what else he'd discover about her when she finally realized how much they belonged together.

When she exhaled, her soft breath drifted across the narrow space between them like a scented breeze. The small sigh that escaped her seemed to be a sound of regret.

Was she dreaming this was their wedding night and she'd lost an opportunity to make passionate love with him? He sure as hell was.

He wanted Laura in his arms in the worst way. He ached to explore every inch of her delectable body, to make love to her, to bury himself in her warmth and to forget there was a world with all its uncertainties waiting for them.

If Laura expected him to wait to consummate their marriage until she got used to him, she was in for a surprise. Not only was she obviously a woman with strong desires of her own, sleeping on his own side of the bed with a chaste wife was more than any man could handle.

What better way was there to get to know each other than to have him make love to her?

And how in the hell was he expected to sleep in the same bed with her and to keep his arms off her without going crazy?

Sleep was slow in coming, but when it did, he dreamed of holding Laura in his arms and making mad, tantalizing love to her.

THE UNACCUSTOMED FEEL of a hard male body holding her awakened Laura. She found herself nestled in Tom's heat. A masculine arm was wrapped around her, a hand was cupping her breast, one muscular leg was holding her captive.

She gave in to an impulse and leaned over and kissed him. Embarrassed, she quickly retreated and glanced at his eyes to see if he was awake. But he was still asleep.

When he whispered her name in his sleep, his warm breath brushed her cheek. The worry lines creasing his forehead spoke of an uneasy dream. A tenderness, coupled with regret swept over her. She lay there, content to be in his arms. When he awakened, there would be time enough to talk about the future.

She lay back against the pillow, watching him sleep and wishing things had been different.

The first rays of sunlight were beginning to shine through the bedroom curtains when she felt him stir. There was a short silence, a hesitation and a muttered oath when he must have realized he was holding her.

"Sorry about that," Tom said, drawing away and wiping sleep from his eyes. "I must have been dreaming." Yeah, of making love to her. Too bad he hadn't been awake to enjoy it, he thought ruefully, since loving her had been all he'd been able to think of lately.

"How do you feel this morning?" he asked, bracing himself for a lecture.

"I feel wonderful," she answered with a small, happy smile. "I haven't slept so well in years."

"Me, too," he said. He would have enjoyed the night more if he could remember if his embracing Laura had only been in a dream. Since she didn't seem angry, maybe she'd enjoyed his unconscious embrace.

He stored the thought for future reference.

He looked over her shoulder to where the curtains hung in silent folds in the morning's stillness. "I hate to say this," he sighed, "but I'm hungry as a bear."

"Today is Sunday," she protested. "There's no reason to get up so early, is there?"

He shook his head. Didn't she know what having her in bed next to him wearing that alluring outfit was doing to him?

"It's too cold to get up," she added burrowing under the blankets with a lazy smile. "Can't we sleep in?"

"Sleep?" he asked hopefully.

"Yes, sleep. At least until the heat kicks in."

If she only knew, the heat inside him had kicked in long ago.

He'd had more than enough of practicing self-control for one night, he thought, mentally checking his condition and hoping Laura hadn't noticed his arousal.

"Sorry, I'm a morning person," he answered, firmly closing his mind to what he couldn't have. "Besides, I really am hungry."

"I suppose I could be persuaded to make you breakfast."

It wasn't breakfast he was hungry for. He leaned on one elbow and stared down at her kissable lips. "What do I have to do to persuade you?"

"If you turn up the heat, I promise to feed you," she answered softly.

The heat was up, he thought as he stared into her eyes.

He waited for her to say something more, but she lay there cozy in her cocoon of blankets looking up at him without moving. He mentally checked the state of his "equipment" again. So far, so good, but he wasn't going to be able to take much more of this.

"Something wrong?" he asked.

"No," she answered. "I was just thinking what a nice surprise it is to wake up in the morning and find you here. And that we would be having breakfast together."

Tom wanted to believe it wasn't food they were talking about. Gazing down into her glowing hazel eyes, dark with passion, he knew she was no practiced flirt. She may have been married before, but she didn't seem to understand what she was doing to him with her on-again, off-again husband-and-wife scenario.

He kissed the tip of her nose, and when she didn't protest, he kissed her lips. He gathered her into his arms and was about to lower her nightgown to kiss her creamy skin and tantalizing breast when a small sigh escaped her.

Was she about to give in to the passions that had overtaken them? he wondered. Would she regret it if she did?

Laura had asked him to wait to consummate their marriage, but he remembered he hadn't gotten around to actually promising anything. Still, a promise between a husband and wife was a promise even if he hadn't exactly voiced it in so many words. He didn't want her to hold this morning's seduction against him.

He couldn't lie to himself. This *was* a seduction. He was so on fire with the need for her, he had been about to take her in his arms and coax her doubts away.

With a last, long kiss, he forced himself to slide from under the covers and to tuck them back around her.

He was heading for the bathroom to dress when he saw her wistful look reflected in the dresser mirror. Maybe he shouldn't have given up so soon.

He started to turn back, then decided to be smart and quit while he was ahead. He was man enough to be secretly pleased he had made some inroads in Laura's defenses.

Chapter Twelve

Showered and dressed in green slacks and a soft white chenille sweater, Laura paused in front of the bathroom mirror. She looked like a bride the morning after a night of passionate lovemaking.

What would Tom say when he saw her, she wondered, blushing anew. Would he tease her or take her in his arms to finish what he'd started?

A pang of desire swept through her at the thought that he was in the kitchen waiting for her. She couldn't wait to tell him she'd decided not to put off becoming his true wife. She wanted to wake up each morning in his arms.

When had she fallen in love with her husband?

Blushing, she hurriedly washed her burning face with cool water.

She found Tom in the kitchen reading the morning newspaper. Her heart raced at his appearance. He was dressed in khaki twill slacks and a form-fitting dark-brown knit turtleneck that clung to his muscular chest. His hair was rumpled as if he'd been running his fingers through it, a sure sign of his frustration. A cup of coffee and a half-eaten cookie were beside him on the table.

Something in the newspaper was troubling him.

"Ready for breakfast?" she asked cheerfully. When he didn't answer, she leaned over his shoulder to scan the newspaper.

"Finding anything good in there?"

"Yes and no," he answered absently.

"Tell me the good part," she said, inhaling the scent of strong, black coffee and chocolate cookies. "I feel so wonderful this morning, I don't want anything to spoil it."

She'd been flying on cloud nine since she'd realized how much she loved Tom. He wasn't even aware of her happiness. Had she read more into their brief exchange this morning than he'd intended? Had it meant more to her than it had to him?

Uncertain of herself when he didn't look up or acknowledge her presence in the way she'd hoped, she drew back.

"The good news is that it's snowing in the mountains, and they're predicting a white Christmas," he answered, still absorbed in the paper. "I'll have to get out the tire chains for the drive up to the cabin."

His distraction told Laura the weather wasn't the information that held him glued to the newspaper. She had to force herself to ask, "And the bad news? Is something wrong?"

"Sort of," he answered. Judging from the frown on his face, the news was more serious than his "sort of" managed to convey.

She'd asked Tom to be honest with her, but somehow she had a premonition the truth wasn't going to be something she wanted to hear. If she backed off now, though, he might never share the truth with her again. "Maybe you'd better tell me that part, too," she said quietly.

He turned and gazed at her for a moment. "It looks as if the rumors about the Eden Clinic are true." He paused and took a deep breath. "State investigators have found enough evidence of unethical medical practices to begin scheduling preliminary hearings into the matter beginning next month."

The last shreds of her contentment gone, Laura dropped into a chair. Her heartbeat quickened. Her newfound euphoria fled, and she sensed her deepest fears were about to come true. Would they find the proof that she wasn't Carly's biological mother? Would the investigators decide that, as a clinic employee, she'd been in on the scam?

What if Jody went public with her claim to Carly?

"So soon?" she said, trying to calm her pounding heart. "I was hoping it would take months to sift through the files. By then, most of the adverse publicity surrounding the clinic would have been forgotten."

"Not with so many of the former patients demanding to know the truth about their infertility treatments," he answered. "According to what I see here, they're lining up by the dozens."

"Sometimes I blame myself for not looking into my own records all these years," she said, gazing into his eyes. "I should have been more curious, but I had no idea that the doctors had their own agenda."

"Don't blame yourself, Laura. No one else suspected it, either." Tom shoved the newspaper aside and eyed his cold coffee. He grimaced and headed for the coffeepot. "At least, not until a disgruntled employee blew the whistle. And I don't see how anyone could possibly accuse you of being involved," he said, as if he'd read her mind. "You're going to be fine." He bent and absently kissed her upturned face as he passed. "Just remember you're not alone in this. You have me now."

"But what if Jody…"

"If it comes to that, I can take care of Jody," he answered grimly. "But it's probably too early to start worrying about her. We don't know if she intends to become involved in the investigation or if she's in this on her own." He emptied the cold coffee into the sink and refilled his cup. "Coffee?"

She shook her head. "No, thanks. I'm more interested in what you think Jody will do."

"What do you say to our going to your office and getting to the bottom of this?"

Laura's fears came thundering back. How could Tom ask her to provide the records that might prove she'd been a surrogate mother? That Carly was some other woman's child?

Tom drifted back to the table and glanced down at the newspaper. "As far as I'm concerned, it doesn't make any difference what Jody does. If things should come to a head, now that we're married, I have as much of a claim on Carly as she does, or better. Just as I have with Beth."

Laura froze. How could she have forgotten the reason for their marriage?

How could she have let herself fall in love with Tom?

Had last night and this morning been more lies in a series of lies?

She gazed at the husband she had decided she loved and could trust. She blamed herself for responding to his magnetic sexual attraction, his kisses, his promises and everything about him that had swayed her senses. Most of all, she blamed him for using her growing desire for him against her, and herself for loving him.

Tom shoved the newspaper aside. "What's the matter? You look as if you've seen a ghost."

"I have," she answered bitterly. "Not that I expect you to care or to understand."

He caught his breath. "Try me."

"I think you've been using me to get Carly," she answered angrily. "That you've been scheming to take her away from me from the day after we first met. And now that you've married me to get her, you think you're home free."

His eyes darkened. "Is that why you wouldn't sleep with me last night?" When she didn't answer, he grew angry. "Dammit, Laura! How can you believe I'm capable of such a thing?"

"That was just more of the charade you've been putting on for my benefit." She fought back her heartbreak, unwilling to show him how deeply he'd hurt her. "I don't believe you've ever really cared about me."

He pushed the newspaper to the floor and leaned across the table. "You can't seriously believe I don't care for you, not after we spent the night together without my touching you. If I'd wanted to take advantage of you, I could have easily managed to do it.

Or this morning. Hell, I was stupid enough to try to keep to our agreement to wait, but—pardon me for being brutally frank—I knew damn well you wanted me inside you as much as I wanted to be there! You know damn well you wouldn't have stopped me, either.''

She made a sound of protest.

"And as for marrying you to get Carly, that's utter nonsense and you know it. I care for Carly and what happens to her.''

"You're too good to be true!" she retorted. "You didn't even know she existed until two short weeks ago.'' She picked up the front page of the crumpled newspaper and shoved it at him. "You're every bit as guilty as Jody is, but at least she's open and honest about what she wants. You married me so you wouldn't have to wait to find out who Carly's parents are.''

Their gazes locked. Laura blurted out her worst nightmare. "For all I know, you and Jody could be in this together!''

"Never!" He tried to take her hands in his, but she pulled away. "Laura, you've got it all wrong! My motives haven't changed. I suggested we could marry and present a united front if and when things came to a head. I swear I only wanted to make sure no one could take Carly away from you and to keep the girls together.''

Now more than ever Tom regretted asking Len to find a way to check the clinic's lab records. Not when he really hadn't needed proof he was Carly's father. He'd known it almost from the first!

If Laura doubted his motives, what would she think of him if she found out?

She shook her head. Her hazel eyes filled with angry tears. "The way things are adding up, I don't think I can believe you."

Angry and frustrated, Tom regarded her in stony silence. "Frankly, after what happened between us this morning, I was sure you wanted me for your husband."

When she blushed and looked away, he knew the argument was over. "I guess we'll just have to wait and see what the future brings, won't we?" he said quietly.

Tight-lipped, she nodded and glanced down at her clenched hands. They *were* married. Short of getting an annulment, a thought as unthinkable as that of exposing Carly to a custody battle, she had to go along with him.

Tom sighed. Ever since he'd met Laura, it had been one step forward in their relationship and two steps back. How was he ever going to convince her he loved her? "If nothing I say will make a difference, I guess we'll have to take it from here. Is there anything I can do to help with breakfast?"

"Later," Laura answered. "I think I hear the girls."

"Laura, wait up!" he called when she swept by him and hurried out the door.

Behind her, she heard Tom push back his chair and jump to his feet. She didn't care. After he'd reminded her how she'd made a fool of herself last night and again this morning, she couldn't go back and face him. She couldn't pretend things were normal between them—not when her world was crashing around her.

She heard the girls before she opened the bedroom door and found them curled up together in one bed. The kittens were wrestling each other on the rug.

"Good morning, Mommy," Carly said happily. "Isn't it wonderful to have Beth living with us? Now we can play together all the time."

"Yes, sweetheart," Laura answered as she forced a smile. Gazing at their happy faces, she realized at least one good thing had come with her marriage to Tom: Beth and Carly were united.

Beth looked up at her with a shy smile. "Now that we're all married, and Carly is my sister, can I call you Mommy, too?"

"Of course, if you're sure that's what you want," Laura answered, sitting down on the edge of the other bed. "But what about your mother?"

For a moment Beth looked doubtful before she brightened. "I can call her Mother, and you Mommy."

Touched, Laura answered, "That sounds like a good idea." At five going on six, it was clear Beth cared more about her mother's feelings than her mother cared about hers. And Laura also knew that Beth was very fond of her. Another reason for she and Tom to remain husband and wife for now.

She picked up the kitten who had been nipping at her toes and buried her face in its soft fur to hide the tears that shimmered in her eyes. It squirmed away and licked her nose.

"Mommy," Carly giggled. "I think the kittens are hungry."

"It sure looks that way, doesn't it?" Thank God for the children, Laura thought. In their innocence, they managed to lighten the atmosphere. "Why don't you girls put on your robes and slippers and come into the kitchen where you can feed them?"

The kitchen, with Tom waiting for her, was the last place Laura wanted to be, but she couldn't avoid him—not when they were going to be living in the same house and, for now, sleeping in the same bed. As angry as she was with him, his magnetism was still overwhelming.

She found Tom pacing the kitchen floor, cautious eyes on the door.

"Good morning, Daddy! Isn't this cool—all of us living together in the same house?"

"Yes, pumpkin, it sure is." With a sidelong glance at Laura, he smiled at Carly. "What would you like to have me call you?" he asked. "Don't you have a nickname?"

He heard Laura mutter under her breath and glanced over to where she was mixing pancake batter so vigorously it splattered on the floor.

"Her name is Carly," she said firmly. "She was named for her father, and I intend to keep it that way."

"Sure thing," he answered with a wink at the startled kids. "Now what?"

"Carly," Laura said, ignoring him, "get a bowl and pour some milk for the kittens. When you're through, you and Beth can set the table. Breakfast will be ready in a minute."

While she busied herself pouring pancake batter

onto the hot buttered grill, Laura could feel Tom's questioning gaze boring into her back.

"The weather report says it's snowing up in Big Bear. How would you girls like to come home with me and check to see if Beth's snow clothes will fit you both?" she heard him ask.

Absorbed in the kittens, the girls agreed. There was a pregnant pause. "Laura, why don't you come along, too? We could make a day of it, maybe buy the provisions we'll need for the cabin."

Laura hesitated. She wasn't anxious for Tom's company but considering the way she doubted his motives, could she let Carly out of her sight?

"No thanks, you go on with Beth. Carly and I'll wait here for you. I'm sure she has enough warm clothing."

"Why can't I go too, Mommy?" Carly's voice quavered.

"Not without me," Laura answered. "I have too many things to get ready around here, and you can help me."

"Come on, Laura," Tom interjected. "We won't be gone that long. When we come back, we'll all pitch in and help."

Laura surveyed the three unhappy faces looking at her. What good could come out of her anger except to make the children unhappy?

"All right," she answered, her gaze intending to tell Tom she was only agreeing for the children's sake.

TOM FROWNED at the sight of a rental car in front of his house. A car with a San Diego license—Jody's.

It was too late to turn around and go back without getting flak from the girls. Maybe it *was* time for Laura to meet Jody. After all, Laura had just as big a stake in this as he did.

"Laura," he said hesitantly, "it looks as if Jody is inside the house. Do you want to turn back, or shall we have it out with her?"

For Laura, the missing piece of the puzzle fell into place. Tom had had a visitor at the convalescent home—Jody! "Was it Jody at our wedding reception yesterday?" When Tom reluctantly nodded, she took a deep breath. "I thought so. Was that when you both planned this meeting? Is that why you brought us here today?"

"Dammit, Laura, that's enough!" He glanced in the rearview mirror. As usual, whenever he and Laura argued, the kids drew together. "If you knew me better, you'd realize I'd never do anything like this behind your back."

"Maybe that's the problem," she answered tightly. "I *don't* know you! But I don't intend to argue about it now. Let's go inside. Maybe it *is* time for me to meet your ex-wife."

Tom pulled into the driveway and parked beside the rental car. By the time he'd helped Beth and Carly out of the back seat, Laura was waiting at the front door with a determined expression on her face. It was a clear sign she was ready to fight for her own.

Tom unlocked the door and held it open. "Beth," he said quietly, "I want you to take Carly and go to your bedroom. Don't come out until I call you. Okay?"

"Okay, Daddy," she whispered, "but I'm scared."

"Don't be, pumpkin. Everything is going to be okay."

Jody was waiting for them in the living room.

"Don't you dare ask me what I'm doing here!" she said defiantly when Tom led the way into the room. "I told you I'd be back and here I am."

Tom's blood ran cold when Laura's accusing look condemned him.

"Jody," he said reluctantly, determined to make the best of a bad situation, "this is my wife, Laura. Laura, this is Jody."

He watched helplessly as Laura studied his ex-wife—feature by feature. He saw her eyes take in auburn curls, the green eyes. The cleft in Jody's chin and the tiny birthmark at the side of her lips.

When it looked as if she accepted the fact that Jody had to be Carly's biological mother, Tom could almost hear the sound of Laura's heart breaking.

The chill of the locked and unoccupied house added to the chill that enveloped him. Was he going to lose Laura after all?

"Why don't we sit down like civilized human beings and talk?" he asked.

"I'm not going to beat around the bush," Jody told Laura, ignoring him. "As I told Tom, I'm going to get married again and my future husband would like to have children of his own. Since I don't know if I can have any more after the problems I had conceiving Beth, I intend to have her with me. At least part of the year." She glanced at the door leading to the back of the house and smiled. "And now that I've finally connected your daughter's appearance with mine and Beth's, I've decided that my fiancé would be even happier with two children around the house.''

"I told you, over my dead body!" Tom burst out. "I don't know if your fiancé is father material, but I know damn well you're not much of a mother!''

"Maybe that was because you were never around to help!" Jody challenged. "Things have changed, and so have I.''

Tom kept his silence. Guilty as charged. Jody wasn't all wrong; he hadn't been a very attentive husband or father. He told himself it had been because of Jody's continual arguments, but maybe he'd been as much at fault as she had. He'd made sure he'd been gone on assignment more often than he'd been at home when he should have worked harder at making their marriage work. Maybe he wasn't marriage material, either.

But she was right about one thing: things were different now. Now that he had a second chance, he wanted a family life of his own so badly he could taste it. He wasn't going to let Jody take that away from him.

"Maybe so," he finally answered, "and, for what it's worth, Jody, I'm sorry. But it's a little late to turn back the clock. As it is, Beth doesn't know you. As for Carly—"

"Carly is *my* daughter," Laura broke in. "As far as I'm concerned, neither of you have a claim on her," she added fiercely, glancing at Jody then fixing her gaze on Tom. "Nothing is going to change that, not even our marriage yesterday."

Tom felt the depth of a despair he'd never felt before. No matter what he'd said, it was obvious Laura still believed he and Jody had planned this meeting.

What did he have to do to prove he'd told her the truth? What did he have to do to show her that he'd fallen in love with her and that he would never willingly hurt her?

He turned his gaze on Jody who stubbornly looked as if she wasn't going to take no for an answer. That didn't come as a big surprise. She'd never taken a no before and, at least in that respect, she hadn't changed.

"You might as well know I've consulted an attorney," Jody said defiantly. "He's advised me to become acquainted with both girls until there's a hearing. And I intend to do just that!"

"You've already sought legal advice?" Tom hadn't dreamed Jody would move so fast. If she'd been advised to get close to the girls, sure enough there was going to be a hell of a lot of trouble ahead.

"Yes," she answered defiantly. "Besides, if you give Beth a chance, maybe she'll want to spend some time with me. As for the other one—" she glanced at Laura "—this Carly, if she knows the truth, she might want to know her real mother."

"Knock it off, Jody," Tom said, moving to Laura's side and laying a warning hand on her arm when she started to speak. "We've had more than enough for now. No one is going to say Laura isn't Carly's mother. Not if I have anything to do with it. As for Beth, I was willing to allow some sort of visitation arrangement between you if that was what she wanted, but not now. I don't care if you've consulted an attorney. I don't like to be threatened. And especially not about Carly."

"Why don't you bring the girls out here and let

them make the choice? I might be persuaded to re-consider.''

Laura realized that even if she didn't trust Jody's motive, Jody had a good point. And maybe she did have a mother's heart. She knew too well how empty arms feel that long to hold a child of their own. She shook Tom's hand away.

Before she could speak, Jody demanded, ''What are you two afraid of? That the girls might like me?''

''In a pig's eye,'' Tom answered. ''Wake up, Jody. This isn't going to get you anywhere. Go home and marry your fiancé. Maybe you'll have more children. Maybe the problems we had before were my fault.''

''I can't take the chance,'' Jody said. ''I'll make a deal with you. Give me one day with the girls and, if it doesn't work out, I'll leave.''

Tom looked at his new wife. The indecision written on her face was more than he could bear to see. He knew his daughter—nothing Jody could say or do would change Beth's attachment to him and to her new mother and sister. But there were Laura's fears to consider. He couldn't put her through any more agony than she was already suffering now that she had to have realized Jody was Carly's biological mother.

''No deal,'' he answered. ''We'll take our chances and wait for the courts to decide.''

''I'm through talking,'' Jody replied with an angry look at Tom. ''I'll see the both of you in court.'' She gathered her belongings and stormed out of the house.

Jody's frustration was so strong, Tom felt it. If she actually wanted a child, he was sorry for her. But Laura, the wife of his heart, was more important. He had to convince her he hadn't been in league with Jody. Somehow, he had to earn her trust.

"Daddy, look at me!"

Tom reluctantly tore his eyes away from Laura and turned to the door. Beth was standing in the doorway looking like a rag doll wearing a coat whose sleeves and hem were inches too short. "Don't I look funny?" she giggled.

"You sure do, pumpkin," he answered. It took all of his willpower to concentrate on Beth and to put the stone wall that stood between him and Laura aside for now. "I guess that means a visit to the mall for some new clothes." He pretended to be sorry. "That's too bad, I know how much you hate shopping."

"Don't be silly, I love to go shopping, especially at Christmastime," Beth answered with a fresh burst of giggles.

"Me, too," Carly said shyly.

"What do you think, Laura? Shall we take the girls shopping for new snow clothes?"

"Can we visit Santa Claus, too?" Beth asked.

"I suppose so," Laura said reluctantly. At least the break would give her a chance to rethink her earlier suspicions of Tom's motives. He couldn't be the guilty man she'd thought him to be or he wouldn't have stood up for her to Jody. Even though he must have known Jody would try to get even with him, he'd turned down his ex-wife's request to see the children for her sake. Maybe she *had* been wrong about him.

THE MALL was decorated for the holidays. At one end, there was a huge Christmas tree decorated with glittering silver garland and red, gold and green light-bulbs. At the top stood an angel, with arms spread wide in a Christmas blessing. Colorfully wrapped boxes were on the fake mound of snow under the tree.

At the other end of the mall, there was a giant iron menorah with eight colored glass candles and one intended to be the watchman who would watch over them during the eight days of the Hanukkah celebration. Blue and silver boxes were stacked underneath.

The loudspeakers were playing Christmas carols. Santa was patiently listening to a long line of earnest little children each with their own wish list.

"Would you girls like to talk to Santa? That is, if you think you're not too old," Tom teased.

"Yes, yes!" Carly and Beth answered and ran for the end of the line.

Laura's heart melted at the tender expression on Tom's face as he watched the girls make their way to Santa's lap. She wondered what he was thinking about.

As for herself, she would have asked Santa to make sure no one could take Carly away from her. And, she thought wistfully, if she had a second wish, it would have been to have Tom love and cherish her for herself.

She watched silently while Beth whispered in Santa's ear. He turned his gaze on Carly, then motioned her forward. The three were lost in conversation until Santa whispered back, nodded, handed them each a coloring book and crayons and the girls moved on.

"Well, pumpkin, it sure looked as if you two had a long list of wishes for Santa to fill," Tom laughingly said when they rejoined them. "Did you leave any wishes for anyone else?"

"We did," Beth assured him solemnly. "We asked Santa to let Carly and me be sisters forever. And for you and Mommy Laura to always be our mom and dad."

"We already are your mom and dad," Tom answered, surprised. "What made you think we're not?"

"Because my mother said so and made you angry and made Mommy Laura cry."

Realizing as never before that small children tended to be frank, Tom gathered the girls to him and glanced at Laura who listened with tears in her eyes. "I guess you both must have heard more than we wanted you to hear, didn't you?"

Carly nodded. "We tried not to, but you were all hollering. I don't mind meeting Beth's mother if you want me to, but I don't want anyone to take us away."

"No one will, I promise," Tom told her. He kissed her cheek and with another hug gently pushed her to her mother. "You, too," he told Beth with another hug. "You both are going to be our little girls until you grow up and two lucky princes will want to marry you."

Laura listened to the conversation, her heart aching. How wrong she'd been about him. If any man was cut out to be a father, it was Tom with his tender, loving ways. And, if time proved she wasn't Carly's biological mother, at least she could do something to ensure that Carly would have her biological father to watch over her.

Chapter Thirteen

"Lunch?" Tom asked when he noticed Laura's exhaustion. As far as he could see, she was the kind of woman who pushed herself too far, and always for someone else. The preoccupation in her eyes troubled him. He couldn't bear to see her unhappy. "You need a break."

"In a minute," Laura answered. "I have to make a telephone call. Go on ahead and get started, I'll catch up with you."

Tom stared after Laura as she headed for the line of telephones on the wall. What was so important that she would leave Carly with him when she hadn't been willing to let her out of her sight before? And why did she have to make a phone call right now?

The girls were happily eating corn dogs and working through French fries when Laura rejoined them. He expected her to chide him for allowing the girls to eat fast food, and was surprised when she didn't comment. His own appetite gone and his mind working overtime, Tom left coffee and a hamburger turning cold in front of him.

"Mission accomplished?" he asked.

"Yes." Laura absently reached for his hamburger, took a bite, then looked apologetic. "I'm sorry, but I'm starved. It didn't look as if you were going to eat it. You weren't, were you?" she added as an afterthought.

Tom blinked. This was definitely a new Laura. Up until now, she'd hardly eaten much of anything. "No, go right ahead," he answered, enjoying the way she dug into the sandwich. She not only acted as if a weight had fallen off her shoulders, she looked years younger and more attractive than ever. He'd seen her this way before, he thought as he eyed the change in her with appreciation, but not often enough to suit him.

Right now Laura resembled the woman he'd first seen in the school auditorium weeks ago, happy and friendly. Until they'd gone backstage and a dark cloud of suspicion had come between them. To his surprise, even that cloud seemed to have lifted this afternoon.

His wandering thoughts took him back to the Eden Clinic and his first instinctive impression that Laura knew more about its operation than she'd been willing to let on. He'd been sure she was hiding something, and, after he'd seen the newspaper headlines, he'd even suspected she might have known about the clinic's unethical operation.

Until he found himself falling in love with her and realized she wasn't guilty of anything but being a mother protecting her child.

"What exactly did you have in mind for the rest of the afternoon?" he asked, suddenly wishing for a honeymoon with all the time in the world to kiss the corner of her lips and touch her creamy skin.

"I've asked Dina if we could drop off the girls for the afternoon," she answered, finishing the rest of his sandwich.

Tom was intrigued.

Carly and Beth looked curious.

"*Both* girls?" he asked with heightened interest.

"Yes," she answered. After a quick glance at the French fries, she took two and munched thoughtfully.

Tom studied her, wondering if he'd heard her correctly. "*Both* girls?" he repeated.

"Of course."

"Did you have something special in mind?" he asked politely, hoping against hope she was going to suggest a reconciliation for just the two of them.

"Errands," she said, shooting down his leaping instincts.

Before he could question her about her cryptic comment, she added, "Just the two of us."

The idea of being alone with Laura for any reason sounded damn good, Tom thought as his senses warmed. Possibly he could find out why she'd been so angry with him. It took him all of two seconds to take her up on her offer. "Eat up, ladies. If you have any more shopping to do, now is the time."

An hour later, loaded with packages, Tom pulled up in front of the Applegate home. Laura put her hand on his when he turned off the motor. "Wait here, please. I'll be right back. We don't have much time."

Time? Time for what? Tom wondered as he released the door locks. He enjoyed mysteries, but only when he was a player. Today, he felt more like an invited silent guest.

Beth hung back. "Aren't you coming in, Daddy?"

"Not now, pumpkin," he said with a close look at his adorable if mystifying wife. "Don't forget to tell your Aunt Dina hello for me. I'll see you later."

He watched Laura take the girls to the door, speak to her sister and hurry back.

"What's so important?" he said as she slid in beside him. "You haven't been yourself all day."

"I guess I have a lot on my mind," she answered quietly.

If Tom had figured she'd start talking now that they were alone, he'd been mistaken. He put the car in gear and turned on the motor. "Where to?"

"The clinic."

"The Eden Clinic?" he asked, turning to stare at Laura. The destination was the last place he'd figured she'd be headed for. "Why? The last time I checked, it was off-limits."

"Not to me," she answered, meeting his gaze squarely. "I have a top secret pass."

Momentarily speechless, Tom couldn't believe his ears. After all her denials and his thwarted need to get into the clinic records, she'd actually been able to gain entry to the clinic any time she'd wanted to! "A top secret pass?"

"Yes."

"Correct me if I'm mistaken," he said slowly as all his earlier suspicions came home to roost, "but didn't you tell me no one, including you, had access to the clinic and its records when I tried to persuade you to let me see them?"

"I had my reasons," Laura answered as she settled back in her seat. She gave him a look that told him that was all he was going to get out of her.

"That tears it!" he exploded. "What do you take me for, a fool? I want to know what changed your mind. Or why you lied to me in the first place?"

"I didn't know you then," she answered, eyeing him placidly.

"And you think you know me now?"

"Yes," she answered, sitting back in her seat. "I do."

"So," he answered facetiously, "am I to take it that now your reasons have changed, you're going to let me in on what's going on?"

"Yes," she answered glancing at her watch, "but I don't think we have time to discuss it now. Can we get started?"

Tom intended to make her understand that, while she may have the upper hand for now, he wasn't through with her. He was going to delve into her mysterious errand whether she wanted him to or not. "Sure, but don't get the idea I've given up on you. I want some answers and damn soon," he added firmly.

"Of course," she answered with a sidelong glance. "Later."

Tom drove to the clinic in a state of confusion. Laura's hot-and-cold behavior of the past few days was beyond logic. Reluctantly shoving the fewer-than-he-would-have-liked hot episodes from his mind with difficulty, he tried to look for answers in the cold episodes.

Earlier this morning, she'd made it clear she didn't trust him farther than she could throw him. Now, only hours later, it was an entirely different scenario with him included as a partner in some scheme she had cooking. What had happened to change her mind? This business of finally knowing him didn't add up. As far as he was concerned, he was the same man he'd always been.

He parked in front of the clinic steps. If Laura had a top secret pass, he wasn't going to pussy-foot around and hide the car. And he wasn't going to let her out of his sight, either.

A burly guard stepped in front of them when they opened the heavy glass door. "Sorry, ma'am, sir, you can't come in here."

Laura flashed an employee pass plainly marked Security Clearance in red letters. "I came back to pick up a few personal belongings," she told the man with a dimpled smile. "I won't be long."

The guard smiled back.

Tom had to admire Laura's performance.

The man studied the pass, checked her against its photograph and made an entry on a clipboard. "Okay, Ms. Edwards, but I'll have to take a look at what you bring out," he said apologetically. "Just routine, you understand."

"Of course," she answered and started briskly down the hall.

"Sorry, sir. You'll have to wait here until Ms. Edwards comes out," the guard said stepping in front of Tom. He gestured to a sofa just inside the door. "You can wait for the lady over there. You're not going in without a pass. Just following orders," he added when Tom glared at him.

Tom protested he was Laura's husband, and was frosted when it didn't do him a damn bit of good.

Maybe the man was only doing his job, but Tom still recognized opportunity when he saw it. The guy must have been new, or he wouldn't have let anyone inside the clinic, not even the husband of an employee with a secret clearance.

A phone rang.

Tom waited until the guard answered his cell phone, gestured to him to stay put and began a tour of the building before he made his move. Putting his years of undercover work to good use, he quickly made for the door next to the one marked Records where Laura was undoubtedly doing her thing.

As the records librarian, Laura knew there were backup disks for each hard disk behind the sealed door in her office. Kept for emergencies, they were located in a safe hidden behind the files. She turned on her computer, and using a special code, entered her name and memorized the file number of the disk containing her treatment records.

Her hands halted in midair when she heard a noise. She listened carefully. When the noise wasn't repeated, she entered Tom's and Jody's names and memorized their file number. Repeating the number under her breath, she pressed a hidden mechanism in one of the tall stacks of files behind her desk. The stack slid open to reveal a safe. She was in the midst of punching in a secret code when she heard another sound.

"Ms. Edwards? Are you in there?" The doorknob rattled.

Laura hurriedly pressed the mechanism and the stack slid back in place. "Yes, what is it?"

"The gentleman who was with you is missing. I thought he might be inside with you."

Laura unlocked the door and held it open for the guard to look inside. "He's not in here," she said with a frown. "Are you sure he's missing?"

The guard sheepishly explained about having to take a phone call, that he'd gone on his rounds after telling Tom to wait. When he came back he'd found Tom gone.

"My husband is harmless, I'm sure you have nothing to worry about," she answered, knowing Tom was anything but harmless when he made up his mind to do something. And, she thought furiously, now must be one of those times. "Have you checked the men's room?"

"Yeah," he said with a glance around the office. "I guess I'll go look again. Sorry to bother you."

Alone again, Laura quickly reopened the safe, took out CDs and put them down the front of her sweater. Shivering when the cold plastic made contact with her skin, she gathered up enough of her personal things to make her excuse for coming to the clinic today look good. After a last look around, she locked the office door and went back to the waiting room.

"Say, I found your husband," the guard told her. He gestured to Tom's automobile. "Looks like he's out there taking a nap. Guess he was in there all the time I was looking for him." He grinned sheepishly. "I never thought of looking out there."

Laura made her getaway before he asked to see what she'd taken from her office. Just as well, she thought. Nothing in her purse would have been worth going back for.

"Mission accomplished?" Tom asked her when she got in the car.

Laura nodded. He was too calm.

"Going to share it with me?"

"Later," she answered, as she buckled her seat belt and glanced back at the guard standing in the clinic doorway. Afraid that he might call her back to search her bag, she smiled and waved. "Let's get out of here now!"

Tom started the motor and resisted the temptation to tromp on the gas. He slowly pulled out of the parking lot.

"Can't you go any faster?" Laura asked, glancing over her shoulder.

"Not without making it look suspicious," he answered. "And quit looking back. Act natural. We'll be out of sight in a minute."

Laura settled back into the seat. "By the way, the guard came looking for you. He told me you were missing. Where were you?"

"Inside the clinic," he answered, fighting to keep his temper under control. If he had the time, he would have throttled her for putting him through this exercise when they could have accomplished the same thing days ago.

"How could you have been in there? The guard said he saw you sitting in the car!"

"I went inside when the guard made his rounds in case you needed help." he replied with a quick glance through the rearview mirror. "When it looked as if you were okay on your own, I came out here to wait for you.''

They drove for a few minutes before he pulled into a market parking lot and maneuvered the car in between two vans to stay out of sight of the street in case anyone was looking for them.

''Now,'' he said, keeping his voice under control with difficulty, ''are you going to tell me what in blazes you were doing back there?''

''Getting the records you were looking for.''

''Why now?''

''Because I felt I owed it to you.''

''And what did I do to make you change your mind?''

''The fatherly way you are with the girls—both of them,'' she answered. With a shy glance at him, she added, ''And the way you are with me, too.''

Surely standing up to Jody and jeopardizing his custody of Beth deserved some reward, Laura mused. Even if it meant breaking her heart. She was going to give him copies of the clinic's records.

Tom interrupted her thoughts.

''By the way, I saw what you were doing back there,'' he told her in a tight voice that warned her he was on to her.

''How? I didn't see you anywhere.''

''The connecting door to the office next to yours was partially open. I watched you for a few minutes.''

Laura flushed. ''Didn't you trust me?''

''No, not at the beginning,'' he answered. ''Not after I discovered you've lied to me about not being able to get into the records. But, like you said, things are different now.'' He fixed her with a look that sent tiny waves of heat coursing through her.

Laura silently met his eyes. How could she tell him it hadn't been a question of trusting him. He'd already proved himself a good father. His strength, love and devotion to the children, and yes, even to her, had overcome her fears he was the enemy.

How could she admit her hesitation had been for herself?

Laura didn't know how she would be able to bear handing him what might be the actual proof he was looking for.

Up ahead, she noticed a Santa ringing a large bronze bell and accepting donations for the needy. Carly had been the best present of her life, and every Christmas since had been a reminder of the treasure of her miraculous birth. She hadn't been able to bear the thought of losing her or of what a contested birth record could do to Carly. It was bad enough for herself and Tom, but they were adults.

''So, where do we go from here?''

''I need more time to find someplace where we can download the CDs I took from the clinic,'' she said, steeling herself to ignore the questions in Tom's eyes.

There was something in Laura's voice that cooled Tom's anger and made his heart ache for her. Maybe it was the poignancy in her voice and the fact that he understood what giving him the records could mean to her.

He remembered the anguish in her eyes when he'd told her he believed Jody was her daughter's biological mother. And the way she'd ultimately accepted their marriage as a means to keep Jody from claiming Carly for her own.

She was braver than he'd realized if she was willing to give him the proof he needed that he was her biological father. Glancing over at Laura, he vowed he'd never do anything to make her regret her decision.

What would another few hours matter when they both already knew what they would find, he asked himself as he agreed to wait. He wanted to take her in his arms and reassure her that, no matter what secrets were buried in the disks, he wouldn't destroy her dreams, her hopes. He loved her enough to make certain no one could take her child from her.

THE VAN TOM HAD RENTED for the trip to the mountains was loaded with Christmas decorations, presents and provisions for their holiday. When Tom pulled up and parked under a covered overhang, the cabin, high in the San Bernardino mountains east of Los Angeles, was surrounded by pine trees and covered with snow.

"All right, everyone," he said. "I'll unlock the door and we'll unload. The provisions go into the kitchen, the Christmas stuff goes in the living room. You can put your own things in the bedroom with twin beds."

It took two trips to unload the van before Tom decided Laura could benefit from some playtime. He tossed a handful of snow at her. Laughing, she decoyed him into a snowdrift where she took her revenge.

Tom grabbed her and stole a warm kiss. "Your

nose is cold," he said jokingly. "How's the rest of you doing?"

"The rest of me is doing nicely," she answered breathlessly. "Just remember the girls are close by." She glanced pointedly to where the children rolled in the snow like carefree puppies.

"Sorry," he said tenderly, brushing the snow from her cheeks. "I can't keep my hands off you."

"You'll have to," she said primly. "At least until later."

"Later isn't going to come soon enough," he said softly into her pink-tinged ear before he shrugged and helped her to her feet. "Until then, I'll take a rain check. Come on, everyone," he called with a last promising smile at Laura, "let's get organized."

Laura carried a box of Christmas decorations into the living room. Navajo cotton rugs were scattered around the room's pine floor, a large imitation bearskin rug lay in front of the fireplace. Large pillows were stacked on a corner of the rug. Two couches ringed the fireplace with a large coffee table in between. A pine table and chairs filled a corner of the room where a counter separated the living room from a fully equipped kitchen area. Through the open doors on either side of the fireplace, she glimpsed two bedrooms, the large one with a fireplace of its own.

It was the bearskin rug that drew Laura's attention. Mental images of lying in front of a roaring fire in Tom's arms and making love flashed in front of her eyes.

"Give me a minute and I'll light a fire," Tom commented as he joined her, his arms loaded with cut logs and kindling wood.

His eyes followed hers as she stared, mesmerized, at the fur rug. A wide smile slowly covered his face when she glanced up at him. "You're right," he said. The twinkle in his eyes told her he knew what she was thinking.

He dropped the wood in a large wicker basket beside the fireplace and knelt to start a fire. "I promised the kids we would cut a tree this afternoon and set it up tonight. But our turn will come soon, I promise," he assured her with the crooked smile that never failed to make her heart beat faster. "After the girls go to sleep, I'll let you collect a few promises I made you. On the condition," he added softly, "that I can collect a few of yours."

Laura flushed at the sensuous promise in his voice. He'd brought the scent of cold air, fresh snow and pine trees in with him, but the heated look in his eyes sent her body temperature soaring. All the pent-up desire she felt for Tom surged through her in a rising tide. Unable to take her eyes off him, she set the box of glittering ornaments on the table and reached for the collar of her parka.

She hesitated and glanced at the front door. "Are you sure the girls are okay out there?"

"I'm sure. They're back outside, making a snowman, their first," he answered, rising and closing the distance between them. "They're so busy, I'm sure they don't mind waiting for us. For now, we have some time to ourselves to talk. As for later—" he glanced at the fire he'd started "—there's another fireplace in the bedroom. And a matching bearskin rug. Here," he said, smiling tenderly into her blush, "let me help you with that."

Their gazes locked, he undid the button at her throat and gently caressed her neck with strong, sensuous hands that awakened every nerve as they passed over her skin.

He seduced her with the look in his eyes, with the touch of his fingers trailing against her throat. And with the strong, masculine aura that clung to him.

Laura found herself shivering with rising desire.

"Soon" couldn't come quickly enough.

She stood as if mesmerized while he unzipped the parka, turned her around, and drew the jacket off her shoulders. In passing, he caressed the hollow between her breasts and kissed the sensitive spot at the nape of her neck that never failed to excite her.

As she leaned against him, Laura hoped it was only a matter of time before "soon" would become "now."

"The children," she murmured, turning around to clutch his hands. "We have to wait."

Wait! All he'd done since they'd been married was wait, Tom thought sourly. He'd had enough of waiting, and he hoped from the look of longing that had come into her eyes, so had Laura. This was going to be the last time he'd put off making love to her, he reflected. Regretfully, he dropped his hands and pulled on his gloves.

"Want to come along and help pick the tree?" he asked, hoping the cold air outside would cool him off while he could still control his physical reactions to Laura. With her skin so flushed, her gaze so ready, cutting down a tree was the last thing he wanted to do right now. If they'd been alone, she would have been in his arms and they'd be making love in front of a roaring fire.

"I guess so," she answered with a shaky laugh. She put the parka back on and fumbled with the zipper. "I think we need a diversion, don't you?"

"I can think of a better one," he answered, helping with the fastening, "but I guess there's a time and place for everything." He engaged the zipper and solemnly closed her jacket. Reluctant to break the sexual tension between them, he took his time with the button at her throat. "There," he said, with a light kiss on her nose. "Let's get going before it gets too dark to see."

"HOW ABOUT THIS ONE?" Once outside, Tom's ardor cooled considerably as the temperature was dropping to below freezing. He pointed to a six-foot fir tree about ten yards from the cabin.

"Are you sure, Daddy?" Beth answered doubtfully, crooking her head to get a better view of the tree. "It's kind of skinny and lopsided, too."

Tom sighed. He was anxious to get back to the cabin, set up the tree and get on with the day that wasn't short enough to suit him. "Looks good to me," he said. "What do you think, Carly?"

Carly regarded the tree in silence.

"Okay," Tom said, resigned to the inevitable. "Let's keep looking. But remember, the tree has to be on our property." He followed Laura's gaze to a perfectly formed tree ten feet away. "Like that one?"

"Yes," Laura answered, blowing on her mittens to keep her hands warm. "But it seems a shame to cut it down."

"Maybe so," Tom agreed. "But tonight we need a special tree for a very special occasion." He beamed at the question in the trio's eyes. "This is our very first Christmas as a family."

"So it is," Laura said with a happy smile as she drew the girls into her arms. "A very special Christmas."

"Maybe it's been waiting for us," Carly whispered.

Beth silently nodded her agreement.

"I think you're right," Tom agreed with a conspiratorial smile at Laura. "Stand back, ladies."

Tom pulled the hatchet from its protective leather sheath and went to work. "By the time we're through, this is going to be a Christmas we're all going to remember."

The tree cut, Tom hefted the cut trunk to his shoulder, and with Laura and the girls guiding the tree's branches in their gloved hands, they slid the tree along the snow to the cabin door.

"Now let's shake off the snow and I'll get the tree inside."

"There," Tom said with satisfaction once he had the tree standing in a reinforced stand. "I think we should decorate it tomorrow after we've had a chance to rest and relax." He glanced down at Beth and Carly with a look that stilled their protests.

Tom made it through a meal of do-it-yourself muffin pizzas toasted over the fire and hot chocolate before he glanced over at Laura, the question in his eyes clear.

"Beth, why don't I help you and Carly get ready for bed? We have a big day ahead of us tomorrow,"

Laura said with a glance at Tom's approving smile. "Your duffel bags are in the bedroom. When you're in bed, your father will come in to kiss you goodnight."

"Me, too?" Carly asked.

"You bet, sweetheart," Tom assured her. "All you have to do is holler when you're ready, and I'll be there to tuck you both in."

While Laura shepherded the girls into their bedroom, Tom gathered the remains of their dinner, threw it into the fireplace and took the empty mugs into the kitchen to soak until tomorrow morning. He had more important things to do than wash dishes.

Tonight was going to be a special night, if he had anything to do with it, he thought as he listened to the wind hurling snow against the windowpanes and banked the fire in the fireplace.

Once he placed the metal fire screen in front of the fire and assured himself the cabin was secure, he added logs to the bedroom fireplace.

It was long past the time for him to show Laura how much he loved her.

Chapter Fourteen

The waiting game was over.

Tonight belonged to him and Laura.

He lounged impatiently on the bearskin rug in front of the bedroom fireplace, seeing her cherished face in the dancing flames. Her smile was magical, her parted lips beckoned and a world of promise shone in her eyes. He'd wanted to make love to her for days, but never so much as now.

Tom stirred restlessly. The rug had absorbed the heat of the fire, but it was nothing compared to the fire that was raging through him.

The bathroom door opened. When Laura came into the bedroom, in the firelight she was everything he imagined she would be—a bride, so lovely she made his heart sing. Pink-tipped toes peeked from under the blue-and-white confection she'd worn on the night they'd been married. A shoulder strap had drifted downward and lay against a taut breast. Her shining chestnut hair hung in soft waves to her shoulders. Her eyes were luminous, her lips parted in a smile.

He rose to his knees, reached for her hand and guided her slender figure down to join him. "I love you in that nightgown,'' he told her, gently caressing a pink shoulder. ''But I have to admit I've looked forward to undressing you myself.''

''Then do it now.'' Laura's eyes shone with a mixture of love and desire.

''Tonight is going to be a new beginning for us,'' he said as he gathered her in his arms and pulled her close. So close, he could feel the rapid rhythm of her heart against his chest. ''I love you,'' he murmured softly into her fragrant hair with all the depth of feeling he felt for her.

When he laid her down on the rug and slowly slid the satin nightgown to her waist, Laura put her arms around his neck and drew him down over her. With a soft sigh of pleasure, she felt his tongue move sensuously over her lips, seeking entry. ''I love you, too,'' she answered softly, her hands cupping his cheeks. ''More than I thought I ever could.''

His eyes seemed to reflect the heat of the fire, searching, seeking, willing her to forget everything that had happened before tonight. She would. She ached with the longing to become his wife, to have him become her husband. To become one in flesh and love.

She arched beneath him. She told him with her eyes she was his to have and to hold as long as fate would allow. She told him with her lips and her body how much he meant to her.

Drawing his shirt off his shoulders, she ran her hands over his broad muscular chest and down to his waist, impatiently tugging at his belt.

''Better let me.'' With a shaky laugh that betrayed

his passion, Tom let go of her long enough to take off his clothing.

Laura ran her hands over his lean waist and down his hips, down the flesh heated by the fire in the fireplace and the inner heat reflected in his eyes. With whispered words of the yearning she felt for him, she followed him down to the bearskin rug, turned on her back and urged him over her.

He was virile and male, everything she'd dreamed of. He kissed her lips, her throat, the hollow at the base of her throat and, finally, each of her swollen breasts until, mindless with her love for him, she writhed under him.

"Tom?" she whispered, unable to voice her need to belong to him.

"Now, sweetheart, now." He soothed her with a litany of love words as he finally made her his. Mingled with a burst of overwhelming physical sensations, Laura felt a sense of completion.

She'd come home to the man she loved.

AWAKENED BY TOM'S KISS at the nape of her neck, and his murmured "Good morning, love," Laura slowly stirred and turned over to meet his gaze.

"Don't tell me you've forgotten who I am!" He grinned, brushing her hair from her eyes.

"No, not really." Laura smiled sleepily. "It's just that I'm not used to waking to find you in bed beside me."

"Better get used to it. I intend to be here every morning from now on. In the meantime, I guess I'll have to remind you I'm your husband!"

Before she could reply, he gathered her into his

arms, pulled her over his chest and smiled up into her misty eyes.

They lay, bare skin to bare skin. The heat of Tom's desire fanned her own, awakened the memories of a night when all her dreams and desires as a woman had been fulfilled. She kissed his lips, his throat and made her way down his body. The salty taste of his skin rekindled her need for him. She met his knowing eyes, and recalling the wanton response he'd wrought from her, blushed.

"It's okay," he said with a tender smile that sent a thrill through her. "You don't have to be embarrassed. We're married."

"I know," she murmured in between tiny kisses on his chest. "It's just that this is all so new."

"Every moment with you is new," he said, turning with her on the bearskin rug and nuzzling the hollow between her breasts. "I have a feeling we're going to wake up like this every morning."

"This way?" she teased. "Promises, promises."

"Give me a minute to catch my breath, and I'll show you."

WHEN THEY EMERGED from the bedroom, they found the girls fully dressed and waiting for them.

"We made breakfast by ourselves," Carly announced proudly.

"You did?" Laura asked with an anxious look in the direction of the kitchen. "What did you make?"

"Milk and cookies."

Laura smiled at the girls' idea of breakfast. "Are you sure that's going to be enough for you?"

"Yes," Beth answered. "We were in a hurry to

start decorating the Christmas tree so we can go play in the snow.''

"That's okay," Tom said. "The tree can wait until this afternoon." Belatedly, he looked to Laura for approval. He'd promised to treat her as an equal, but he was off to a sorry start.

"You girls have waited long enough," Laura agreed. "But remember, not only is tonight Christmas Eve, I think we also have a couple of birthdays to celebrate, too."

"A real birthday party?" Beth asked hopefully.

"Sort of," Laura answered. "But you'll have to settle for store-bought cake. And tonight you may each open one present."

"Cool," Carly announced, with a happy glance at her new sister. "Now Beth can have a birthday party, too!"

"Does that mean we can go outside now?" Beth asked, edging toward the door. "We already ate while we were waiting for you to get up."

"Just this once," Laura smiled. "From now on you two are going to have a healthy breakfast. You can hang the decorations later while I make popcorn. I thought it would be fun for us to make popcorn garlands for the tree this year."

The girls exchanged dubious looks. "It takes too long."

"I can see the idea doesn't appeal to you," Tom said with a grin. "You kids go on outside, just try to stay out of trouble, okay?"

"Okay!" The girls dashed out the door.

"Coffee?" Laura turned to Tom.

"Sure," he answered. "But cookies aren't going

to do the job—I'm starved.'' He winked at Laura, and opened his arms. ''How about it?''

''Breakfast!'' she answered firmly. ''And then to work.''

THE SCENT OF freshly popped popcorn filled the cabin. The flames flickered on the few ornaments the girls had managed to hang on the tree before they'd opted for playing in the snow a second time.

Tom sat on the floor in front of the fire listening to the happy sounds of the girls making another snowman. Laura softly hummed to the Christmas carols playing on the radio. Contented, he gazed into the fire and thought how fortunate he was to spend a white Christmas in the mountains with a wife he loved and who loved him. And with two wonderful little girls to complete his happiness.

How lucky could one guy get, he wondered silently as he watched Laura threading popcorn.

The kids had been right—it was probably going to take forever to get the popcorn strung, but as long as forever included Laura, it was all right with him. He grabbed a handful of popcorn and popped it into his mouth.

''If you keep that up, we're never going to get all this popcorn strung.'' Laura laughed.

Tom sighed, strung a few inches of popcorn, then popped some more into his mouth.

''Incorrigible,'' Laura chided.

'''Fraid so,'' Tom answered. He took the popcorn garland out of her hands and set it aside. ''We *are* alone, you know. Maybe we ought to put the time to better use.''

"I don't think so, there's too much to do," she said, taking the bowl of popcorn out of his reach. "Maybe next year we'll use cranberries. They don't take so long to string."

Out of the corner of her eye, she studied Tom while he halfheartedly strung a few kernels of popcorn. Her heart was full of love, her thoughts bittersweet. As a measure of her trust and her decision that the DNA results didn't make any difference, she'd made love with Tom before she kept her promise to give him the printout of the records. Still, it was only a matter of time before she had to keep her promise.

Puzzled that he hadn't asked her for the results by now, she made up her mind to give them to him first thing in the morning, before the girls awakened. She couldn't bear the idea of allowing anything to spoil tonight.

The girls came laughing into the cabin, bringing a blast of fresh air and falling snowflakes with them. Laura put aside the popcorn streamers, bundled the girls into a hot shower and into dry clothing.

"Lunch," she announced. "I made sandwiches this morning. Then, we can all finish trimming the tree."

"Not me," Tom said with a groan, "I couldn't eat a bite."

"No wonder," Laura said. "You've eaten more popcorn than you've strung!"

"Guess so." He glanced around the cabin. "On the other hand, what do you say to a picnic?"

"A picnic?" She gestured to the cabin's windows where they could see snow was steadily falling. "It's snowing outside!"

"No problem," he answered, patting the rug beside

him. "We can picnic in our favorite place, in front of the fire."

He grinned when Laura blushed. He loved the way soft, pink color rose from her shoulders to her cheeks. Lord, he thought as they exchanged knowing glances, he'd never have enough of loving her.

"I like this kind of picnic, Daddy," Beth announced as she and Carly helped Laura prepare a picnic table.

"Me, too," Carly said. "Can we do it some more?"

"Every day it snows," Tom agreed. "After lunch, let's finish the tree and you kids can each open a present—we'll count it as a sort of birthday present."

"Cool," they said, bolting for lunch and making for the presents Tom had stacked under the tree. It took them ten minutes of intense concentration before they finally made their choice.

"More Barbies!" Carly said breathlessly. "And clothes."

"Look," Beth said. "There's even a computer for her to play with!"

The girls' excitement was catching.

With time out to decorate the tree and to eat a fried chicken dinner, the girls were busy playing with their dolls for the rest of the day.

Noticing the meaningful look Tom was sending her, Laura nodded. "Okay, girls, time for bed. The sooner you go to bed and fall asleep, the sooner it will be Christmas morning."

Tom couldn't wait.

IN THE DIM recess of dawn, Tom held a sleeping Laura in his arms. Her lips were curved in a soft smile, her cheeks were rosy in the aftermath of a night of love.

He thought of the report Len had managed to get to him before they'd left for the mountain cabin and that he'd put in his suitcase. He hadn't opened it, and didn't intend to. When it came to Carly's biological mother, the only face Tom could see in front of his eyes was Laura's.

If ever a woman was meant to be a mother, he mused as he glanced down at his wife, it was Laura. Only an oversight of nature had turned her into a surrogate mother. With her genuine mother's love for Carly, and now for Beth, he wasn't interested in what any DNA results revealed.

He eased out of bed, threw on a robe and stoked the smoldering logs in the bedroom fireplace. With a smile at his sleeping wife, and the thought that the girls would soon be up, he went into the main room of the cabin and rebuilt the fire in the fireplace.

"Tom?"

He straightened, smiled and reached out for Laura's hand. "Come on, sleepyhead, it's Christmas morning. The kids will be up soon."

Laura shivered and drew her robe closer around her. "Couldn't we go back to bed until it gets warm?"

"The fire is only for show. It's snowing again and I've already turned up the furnace. But if that's not enough," he added as he opened his arms, "come on over here and I'll warm you."

"The girls," she said, as she drifted to his side.

"Yeah, I know," he answered ruefully as he cradled her in his arms and nuzzled her tousled hair. "I guess I'll have to give you a rain check. In the meantime..." He handed her an envelope. "I want to start out by being honest with you. I had a friend of mine check into the clinic's records before I found out you could if you wanted to. Now, the answers don't mean a thing to me. You can open it or not, it's up to you."

"Do you know what's in it?" she asked hesitantly.

"I can guess."

"And I have a gift for you, too," Laura murmured. "I was going to give it to you last night, but you kept me too busy to remember it." She reached into her robe pocket, withdrew an envelope of her own and gave it to him.

"A Christmas present?" he joked, trying to make light of one of the most important moments of his life. And one that showed him how much Laura loved and trusted him to do the right thing. "Where's the red ribbon?"

He knew, as sure as he knew his own name, that Laura had given him the DNA results downloaded from the computer disks she'd taken from the clinic. That her gift to him—actually her sacrifice—was the truth. How could he show her it wasn't the truth that he wanted to hear?

He glanced at the fire, whose flames rose to disappear into the chimney flue. With a reassuring smile at Laura, he threw the envelope into the fire.

"Are you sure?" she asked. When he nodded, she glanced at the envelope he'd handed her and, encouraged by his smile, threw it into the fire. They watched the paper curl into ashes.

"I'm sure of everything that matters," he answered, drawing her to his side. "As far as I'm concerned, biology doesn't make a woman a mother or a man a father," he said softly so that only she could hear.

He reached to wipe away the tiny tears of happiness that appeared at the corners of Laura's eyes. "Now, I could use a cup of hot chocolate."

"Mommy, is it Christmas already?"

"Daddy, did Santa come last night?"

Beth's and Carly's excited voices interrupted Laura before she could answer Tom. To tell him that the envelope had been sealed with her love.

"Santa must have come early this morning," Tom replied with a straight face. "Your presents are under the tree. Your mother and I already have ours."

"Where are they?" Beth asked. "I don't see anything."

"I saw you throw something into the fire," Carly said with a frown. "Didn't you like your presents?"

"Very much," Laura said, her eyes glowing with love. "We gave each other our trust. It was the best presents we could have given each other."

"Now, one question," Tom said, gently turning Laura's face to meet his when the girls glanced at each other, shrugged and went back to their presents. "Will you marry me?"

"I thought we already were married."

"That was because you thought you had to marry me," he replied. "This time I want you to marry me because you want me for your husband—with no strings attached."

"Other than love," Laura amended softly.

Epilogue

Beth Anne Aldrich
and Carly Jane Edwards
Request the Honor of Your Presence
at the Marriage of Their Parents

Laura Beckwith Edwards
and
Thomas Lee Aldrich

Sunday,
the Twenty-Fourth of January, 2000
1:00 P.M.

at
The Oddessy Restaurant
Malibu, California

Reception to Follow

If you enjoyed what you just read,
then we've got an offer you can't resist!

Take 2 bestselling
love stories FREE!
Plus get a FREE surprise gift!

EXTRA! EXTRA!

The book all your favorite authors are raving about is finally here!

The 1999 Harlequin and Silhouette coupon book.

Each page is alive with savings that can't be beat!

Getting this incredible coupon book is as easy as 1, 2, 3.

1. During the months of November and December 1999 buy any 2 Harlequin or Silhouette books.

2. Send us your name, address and 2 proofs of purchase (cash receipt) to the address below.

3. Harlequin will send you a coupon book worth $10.00 off future purchases of Harlequin or Silhouette books in 2000.

Send us 3 cash register receipts as proofs of purchase and we will send you 2 coupon books worth a total saving of $20.00 (limit of 2 coupon books per customer).

Saving money has never been this easy.

Please allow 4-6 weeks for delivery. Offer expires December 31, 1999.

I accept your offer! Please send me (a) coupon booklet(s):

Name: _____

Address: _____ City: _____

State/Prov.: _____ Zip/Postal Code: _____

Send your name and address, along with your cash register receipts as proofs of purchase, to:

In the U.S.: Harlequin Books, P.O. Box 9057, Buffalo, N.Y. 14269
In Canada: Harlequin Books, P.O. Box 622, Fort Erie, Ontario L2A 5X3

Order your books and accept this coupon offer through our web site
http://www.romance.net
Valid in U.S. and Canada only.   PHQ4994R

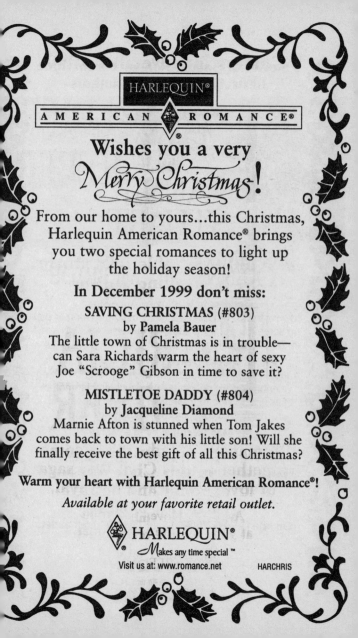

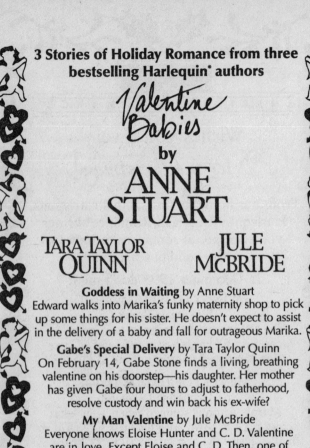